JONATHAN *and the* SACRED SCARAB

SO IT BEGINS!

James Bowlby

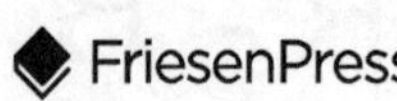

One Printers Way
Altona, MB R0G 0B0
Canada

www.friesenpress.com

First Edition — 2024

ISBN
978-1-03-916014-9 (Hardcover)
978-1-03-916013-2 (Paperback)
978-1-03-916015-6 (eBook)

1. *Young Adult Fiction, Fantasy, Historical*

Distributed to the trade by The Ingram Book Company

This first novel is dedicated to:

My daughter Bronwyn Louise Bowlby,

Who shared adventures with me in Egypt.

PROLOGUE
I'M JUST A BOY

The wind blows powerfully off the Sahara with a plaintive sound, mourning the dead. Mounds of sand mark the remains of buried kings. Dad points out the ruined pyramids to me, but then the wind picks up, rocking the jeep.

I can't even see the corners of the dirt road. I can feel my heart thumping in my chest as the jeep rocks back and forth. It's making me sick. A horrendous gust of wind hits us, and the jeep is tossed off course. Then everything goes black.

I slowly sit up and look around. I'm sitting on broken glass from the back window. Everything seems topsy-turvy: the hood is off the jeep, water is hissing, I smell gas, and the jeep is almost upside-down. I look back and forth; my heart is beating fast. The roof of the jeep and the seats are pushed down, so I'm stuck and I can't get out. I look back. Dad is bent over the steering wheel, bleeding. There is a lot of blood running down his face. My first thought is that he's sleeping on the wheel; that's crazy, I know, but I just can't imagine my dad being hurt.

The wind blows so loudly now that it hurts my ears. I clamp my hands over them as I wonder: *Is Dad going to be all right? And Mum? She also seems to be sleeping in her seat.*

In the blowing sand, I see a strange purple cloud swirling. Well, it's sort of purple. Then *he* is there. I suck in my breath. A strange creature, part muscular man with a long, black rod in one hand and a cross with a handle in the other. His face becomes clear: an enormous black beetle, like a mask. He is ugly, terrifying.

I hear his booming voice like the blowing wind, only his voice is gruffer, and he speaks with clicks. "I am here!"

He raises the cross high above his head, and the wind stops. He says it again, "I am here!" I don't know why, but his words make me relax. I let out my breath. He vanishes in a purple cloud.

The jeep is bent around me, and I realize I need to crawl out. "Dad! Mum!" I yell. My heart thumps loudly. The wind has driven so hard it blew into the jeep. I look at Mum sitting in front of me, but the seat is pushed sideways. Everything is wrong. She seems asleep. There is sand on her.

Then, like magic, her eyes open. "Oh, Jonathan, you're all right, you're all right," she says. "Just breathe slowly. Like you've been taught. We'll get you out." She then calls out, "Help! Help!"

Two men arrive, talking in another language. They pull on the bent jeep door until it falls out towards them. I crawl out.

"Oh, thank you, thank you. I'm free!" I shout.

I turn around to help Mum out. Once free, she pours some water from a bottle onto her scarf and wipes the sand from her eyes and face. She has bright eyes, so clear and blue. They have a special sparkle. I'm so glad she's all right.

I'm sort of glad to be here, but this isn't how I thought it would be. I've seen pictures of palm trees and farms along the Nile. Now all I see is desert. Where is the famous green river?

"Wow, that was something," I tell Mum. I feel dumb saying it.

I want to live up to my parents' expectations. They say I'm bright and I need to show I'm clever. But what if I'm not? I don't always feel smart. I have intelligent people around me most of the time, from Dad's university or Mum's law firm.

"Beth, are you all right?" A friendly bald man says as he comes to help.

"Yes, and so is Jonathan, but Darryl has hit his head. He's bleeding."

I look at the man, whose brow is wrinkled in concern. "What a terrible way to be welcomed to Egypt," he says. His bald head is sprinkled with sand.

"Dr. Czerny, I'm worried about Darryl." Mum is holding back tears. She had been smiling before. I guess the smile was for me.

"Mrs. Johnsten," Dr. Czerny says calmly, "this is Abdoullah. He is part of our team. He saw the accident, got your son out, and called an ambulance. It should be here before long."

Mum nods at Abdoullah.

An ambulance. Does that mean Dad is hurt really bad?

Dr. Czerny continues, "I think you should both be checked over. We have a medic on staff."

"I'm fine," Mum says.

"I insist," the Egyptologist says, smiling. Abdoullah takes me to the medical tent.

In a big tent with hospital beds, a medic takes my temperature, listens to my heart, and checks me all over.

"You're a very lucky young man," he says. "There are just a few bruises starting to show."

Mum comes into the medical tent just as the medic finishes with me. She gives me a pat. I think she's trying not to look worried.

I wander out of the tent to where Abdoullah is waiting for me. "Come with me, Master Johnsten. Let's get you cleaned up of the storm." He speaks differently, and it's clear English isn't the language he usually speaks. He gives me his hand to take. I'm past the stage of hand holding, but today, after being stuck in a jeep that crashed in a new country, I'm glad he offered it. He has big hands.

I walk quickly with Abdoullah, who takes me to the washhouse. I've never even thought of a bathroom being in a tent. I hear the ambulance leave when I'm in the shower. You can hear everything in a tent.

Abdoullah comes into the washhouse with my suitcase. "Your mother and I found your suitcase in the jeep," he says.

I laugh because there is even sand in my suitcase. I shake everything out before I get dressed.

Cleaned up and dressed in fresh clothes, I come out. Looking around the area Dad calls the "dig" or "camp," I see that sand has blown up against the tents. Some tents have blown down completely and look funny propped up by the things inside. Men are busy fixing them.

A man with the darkest eyes I have ever seen comes over. "You must be Jonathan. I heard you were coming. I'm Dr. Gorman. I work here too." His dark eyes and how closely he stands bother me. I know I'm expected say something, but I don't know what it is.

After an awkward moment of silence, Dr. Gorman leaves with a smile. There is something strange about that smile. It's sort of crooked. He spooks me and I'm shaking when he leaves.

The bald man Mum called Dr. Czerny comes over. He's laughing and shaking his head. "Welcome to Egypt," he says smiling. "Always the unexpected," he chuckles. I really like his smile. I smile back.

I look around. I had expected to see the green river Nile, but this place called Saqqara is all dry, with lots of blocks of stone lying around. I watch Mum go over and sit in the shade of one of the few trees. I wave; she waves back. Both of us are glad to be okay.

Dr. Czerny sees me looking around. "It seems like a desert, but it's only about an hour's drive to Cairo. Your father told me you've always wanted to come to Egypt. So, we'll put you to work." I think he's only doing this so I won't think about my dad.

Dr. Czerny is a small man, taller than I am, but I'm only ten. He's lost a lot of his hair but has a great smile and looks strong. I bet he works out or finds lots of hard work to do here.

Dr. Czerny reaches into his bag and pulls out some tools. "Here is a brush and a trowel. Abdoullah is waiting over at the tomb. Do you see him? He'll be your assistant."

We hurry to a tunnel between two piles of rocks. A tall, big-chested, young man comes out to us. It's the first time I look at him properly.

Abdoullah is wearing a long, dark-red, dress-like thing, Dad said it's called a jellabiya, that many men in Egypt wear. I've seen Egyptian men wearing them in my dad's pictures.

"Hello again, Jonathan," he says.

I find it difficult to know what to say. Finally, I say, "Hi."

Dr. Czerny says, "Do you want a job as a young Egyptologist?"

I nod and grin. Of course, I do, but I don't say anything 'cause I'm a bit shy with new people. I'm glad to be going to work in a tomb, though.

"Abdoullah will take you into the pyramid and set you up, Jonathan. If you need anything, he'll help you," Dr. Czerny states.

This is great; it's what I've always wanted to do. For most of my life, I've pestered Dad to tell me about his work in Egypt. Now I have the chance I need to dig, find something in the tomb, and show Dad I'm not just a little kid. It would be cool to find things like gold or jewels. But what if I don't?

I wanted to work alongside Dad, but now he's in the hospital. Before I have time to think much more about him or get too sad, we enter a tomb—a sort of cave-like place. There's a big pile of old bricks on top.

"This being someone's burial pyramid, we needed to look to find the name of the owner. His name was Heka," Abdoullah says.

"This doesn't look like a pyramid," I note.

"It used to be a beautiful pyramid," Abdoullah tells me, "but some later kings came and took the nice stones from the outside and used them for their own tombs. The limestone blocks had to be brought here by boat down the river, so it was easier to re-use some from another tomb."

"I thought kings would have wanted to help other kings, especially their great-grandfathers," I say.

Abdoullah nods and we go inside. Some walls have paintings. There is this beautiful painting of a woman in a long, flowing white dress; her black hair has strips of gold woven into it.

Abdoullah points at the painting. "This is the princess whose father owned this tomb. She is wearing the wig she would wear to court with her father for an audience with the king. Look, there are tables here with bread stacked up and jars and goblets of wine. As well, there are pictures of their servants carrying large plates of food for the man and his family."

Abdoullah takes me down a long, sloped passage. The painters decorated the walls down here like a park—many trees, lots of reeds, and even ducks swimming in the river. We stop. It looks like we're at the end of some kind of room.

"This little space was for statues that are no longer here." Abdoullah bows his head. I think he's sad the statues have been taken away. "They have been taken to the Luxor Museum. One day, we should go there."

We walk further down the passage before stopping once again.

"This next little room is your place to excavate. Dig here and see if you can find anything. I don't think anyone has been excavating here before. Haas Saaid!"

"What did you say?" I ask.

"Haas Saaid! Good luck in Egyptian."

"Haas Saaid! I hope you have good luck too."

I think that by speaking Egyptian, Abdoullah is making me his friend.

I look in my little room. All I see is dirt and dust. I don't see the gold of a king. Pretending, I say, "This is great," and get to work.

Abdoullah encourages me, "I'll be just down at the end of this passage. Yell if you want me."

"What are you doing there?" I ask, curious.

"There's another room, farther along, that we think might be the place of the sarcophagus of Heka. You might see some other men or women come down past your room." Abdoullah again says, "Haas Saaid."

I'm really excited. Dad is a famous Egyptologist and I'm expected to be like him, to find something in this old tomb. I dig into the clay and sand. I wonder how Dad is doing.

I don't see anything but more dirt. I take my trowel and work away. Maybe I will find something. I'll try.

After a while, I get bored. I sit for a few minutes and think about saying, "I give up," but I don't. Finally, I think I see a brief glimmer of something, so I get going again, this time with my brush. I want to find something so they can say I'm a great Egyptologist.

I find a few little pieces of wood; I work with my brush then find some more. It's a broken box, very old and dry and fragile. I see gold strips; I guess they were straps that sort of held the box together. I want to show Abdoullah, so I brush some more and see more of the straps. I'm so excited. I yell, but no one hears me. I feel sad; I want to show someone the box.

After working for a while longer, I just want to get out of this dusty, closed-in tomb, but I'm sure an Egyptologist doesn't say that, so I just keep working. Then I start to breathe rapidly. I'm surrounded by old stone walls that seem to get closer together the more I look at them. I must stop and breathe slowly and deeply. One, two, three. Like I've been taught. It helps and makes me feel like I'm in control. That's what Mum says.

I want to show Abdoullah what I found. I go out into the passage.

"Abdoullah! I found something!" No answer. I can hear Abdoullah working on his own excavation. I walk down the passage and look around the corner.

Abdoullah is down at the far end of the passage. The farther he digs into the dirt, the less I can see him. There is an actual wall on both sides, making the room quite wide. Wider than mine. Then I hear his small trowel strike something solid: stone. I watch him brushing and see a small part of the big, carved, smooth, shiny rock. He has found the sarcophagus. My Dad told me .... I keep saying that.

I better get back to work and see what else I can find. I go to my room and brush away the dirt. I carefully take out the sort of lid. Now I can look inside the broken box. I see part of a rolled-up sheet of Egyptian papyrus. I know it's papyrus because Dad has a picture on a big sheet of it at home. Abdoullah goes by. I call, but he doesn't hear me. The papyrus is wrapped around something special, I bet. I expose the wrapped papyrus. Inside it is something wonderful. It is a smooth stone beetle, no bigger than my hand. I use my brush to clean it off.

I turn it over and see hieroglyphics on the bottom. I'm so proud that I found something. Time has worn it smooth, with white, green, and brown waves in it. As I rub my hand over the beetle, I feel a bit weird. I think maybe the light is changing. Maybe it's the generator? Dad says they're not reliable.

I think this beetle is special, but no one will believe me. I rub it on my shirt. The light in my little room grows brighter than before. A weird, purple, smoky mist slowly fills my space. I feel scared, but I really like this mist. The purple mist thickens until it's a cloud, and then a powerful man appears—the creature I saw in the sandstorm. His beetle face still scares me, so I crouch down, but then I look up at him.

He has big muscles. He looks so weird, but somehow, I get the impression that he's nice. He smiles a bit and I can see his bottom teeth below his beetle face, like he's wearing a living mask. I'm not sure he's supposed to be able to smile, but he does somehow. I wonder if I should get away.

Then I hear his loud, hollow-sounding voice mixed with beetle clicks. "Do not be afraid. I am the God of Youth and New Life. I will protect you. You called me by rubbing the scarab. The God Ra, the most powerful, is with me in spirit. When he joins me, I am called

Khepri-Ra." His voice echoes as he speaks. "My symbol is the beetle, the scarab. You found my Sacred Scarab. It has power. Protect it. Do not let another take it from you. I have directed you here to find it."

I think I hear someone coming. I look to see who it is. When I look back, the strange beetle man has disappeared into his purple light. I feel alone. I felt good when he was here. He's sort of ugly, but I like him. I think he understands me. He said he'll protect me.

I take off my shirt and put the larger sheet of papyrus on it, then I pick up some pieces that had broken off. I carefully add the old wooden box with the gold bands around it and wrap them up in my shirt. I put the scarab in my pocket and crawl out of my spot.

In the passage, the light grows brighter. Why? I have put the scarab away. I realize I have to move back. There are now two big, powerful creatures standing there: my friend Khepri and a jackal-headed god. I don't know if he's a god, but he's built like Khepri, just with a different head.

"The boy is mine!" the jackal-headed one calls as he becomes clearer, coming out of his own grey mist.

"You cannot have him, Set. He already belongs to me," Khepri scoffs. "I know what happens to boys in your collection."

"I will have him!" The jackal-headed god raises a long staff and bangs it. The pyramid shakes. "I will control him, add him to my collection."

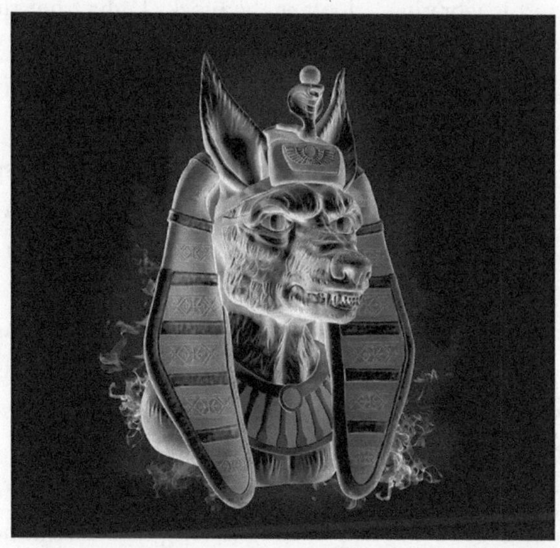

"You behave abominably, horribly, detestably. All the gods turn from you and abhor your actions. Even your wife detests you," Khepri states.

Their arguing is so loud it scares me. Why would they be fighting?

Without warning, Set strikes his WAS sceptre against the ground and there is a tremendous echoing bang. I fall back into my room. A smooth limestone block falls directly on my foot sticking out in the passage. It's so painful I'm screaming, but with the limestone now blocking the doorway, no one can hear me.

All I feel is pain, so I cry. What should I do? I yell, "Abdoullah! Abdoullah!" before curling up to wait. I'm stuck in this little place that's not even a real room. "Help!" I yell. I call for Abdoullah again. No one can hear. No one will come. With the block filling the entrance, I don't even know why I'm yelling.

But I have my scarab! I rub it on my shorts. The beetle-headed god might help. I slowly clean away the grime to show the beautifully carved lines of the beetle. It glows slightly, so I rub a bit more. Now the glow brightens my corner of the tomb.

My hand is vibrating. I look at the block. Light from the scarab shines on the limestone, showing me a deep carving of Khepri. I smile; it's so real. It even has some old paint on it. Khepri was just fighting with the jackal-headed god he called Set.

My leg hurts so much and I'm scared, trapped in this tiny space. My heart beats fast. I breathe like my parents taught me. When I'm in a small space, just breathe slowly. 1, 2, 3. I rub the scarab harder.

"Abdoullah!" I yell. I rub really hard.

My scarab glows brightly, then a rope appears and magically wraps itself around the enormous block, lifting it up. My foot is free but still hurts. I swing my leg away. Suddenly the block crashes back down. I try and stand but I can't walk on my foot. Maybe it's broken.

I hear Abdoullah come. His voice is muffled.

I hear him going for help, calling as he goes. Finally, men come down the passage and take hold of the rope that has wrapped itself around the huge block. Abdoullah yells for the men to pull together. With the strength of all the men pulling on the thick rope, the block begins to slide. I can hear water splashing on the floor in front of the block on the other side. I read that ancient Egyptians used to do this to make the large blocks slide easier.

When the block has moved more than a metre, Abdoullah scrambles over it and into my room. I see him staring at my bloody foot. The men in the passage keep sliding the block.

"You are really brave!" Abdoullah says. "How did you help move the block?" I think he sees my scarab glowing, then going dark. I shove it in my pocket. He picks me up in his muscular arms.

I don't want to tell anyone my secret. "I just waited. I knew someone would come."

"I think," Abdullah ponders for a moment as he carries me, "that you connected to the power of the past. You were able to use the power of the ancient gods."

I look at him. How would he even know that or think to say that? Could he see the light left in the tomb? Did he see my protector, the beetle-headed god?

Abdoullah carries me into the wide passage, past the men pulling on the block and out of the tomb.

Once we're outside, Dr. Czerny takes charge. "Take him to my jeep."

Mum runs up; I didn't know she could run so fast. "Oh Jonathan, are you all right?" She looks at my foot. "Oh my god," she gasps, and covers her mouth with her hand. I guess it's bad. I don't want to look.

Mum climbs in the jeep. Abdoullah puts me in beside her and I rest my head on her lap. I still haven't let go of the little bundle wrapped in my shirt.

Abdoullah drives, and when we get to the hospital, he carries me in while my mother talks to the nurse.

The doctor gives me two pills for the pain then looks at my foot and orders an X-ray. When the X-ray is finished, he reads it and says, "You're a lucky young man. I'm putting a cast on your foot and lower leg so the injury heals straight." He gives me an odd look before he continues. "There's something strange about this accident. Your foot should have been seriously crushed, if it was a huge limestone block like you described." He looks at Abdoullah and shakes his head. "I can't understand it."

Abdoullah looks at me. We exchange a smile.

Abdoullah drives back while Mum sits in the back with me again. I show her what I have in my shirt.

"Jonathan, this papyrus you found looks very important. Dr. Czerny tells me the tomb was built for a scribe who was also a magician."

I tell her, "Abdoullah showed me the picture of his beautiful daughter on the wall of the tomb. I also found this." I show her the beetle. I hope she'll say I've done a good job.

Mum looks stunned. "It's a scarab! Your father told me scarabs bring good luck. When we were at the hospital, the doctor told me your father was lucky, too. He doesn't have a concussion and will be able to leave the hospital tomorrow."

When we get back to camp, Abdoullah carries me to my tent and sets me on my bed very carefully.

"Mr. Jonathan, could you tell me about the scarab?" he asks.

"What about the scarab?"

"I saw it in the tomb, glowing, and a cloud with a strange figure."

"I just dug it up."

"Then what happened to you? Please tell me all."

I look at Abdoullah. Such an honest face. I know I can trust him. He said the scarab is a connection to the ancient past. I think he saw the God Khepri. I decide to tell him,"I rubbed the scarab on my shorts and then this big beetle-headed man with muscles appeared. He said he's the god of young people and he will keep me safe. When the block hit, I called you, but you couldn't hear. I rubbed and rubbed, the scarab lit up, and the block began to lift."

I see recognition on Abdoullah's face. "Keep the scarab safe, little man. It is special. Hide it. Now get better." He looks so serious.

I know I'm special. I've seen a god—two gods—and I've found a sacred scarab.

The next morning, I go with Mum to the hospital. It's a bit of an expedition since Abdoullah has to carry me. Sitting with Dad, I watch him as he scratches his three-day-old beard. I'm amazed it grows so fast. I can tell he's thinking. But what is he thinking about?

"This tomb you were excavating belongs to Ra Nefer Heka. They have not excavated this tomb since its discovery in 1848. The man's name means, 'Proud or happy – 'nefer' in the magic of Ra,' the sun god. Ra Nefer Heka was a scribe or magician. 'Heka' in his name means magic or medicine."

I give him the scarab. "Dad, what does it say on the bottom of this?"

He looks at the scarab, then a look comes on his face like something is wrong. He answers too quickly. "It, ah, promises safety and happiness."

"It brought me luck. I could have been in the passage when the block fell. It's scary to think about that! What does the papyrus say?"

He squints and reads; then his eyes widen, and he replies, "The same as the bottom of the scarab."

Dad doesn't tell me anything more. I think he's not telling me what it really says. Why won't he tell me?

"Dad, please, tell me what it says."

"I'm tired," he says suddenly. He seems disturbed by the scarab. I don't know why he can't just talk to me. I don't think he really is tired.

Back at camp, in my tent, I read and then doze off, my book on my chest. Dr. Gorman visits and wakes me as he comes into my tent.

"What are you reading, Jonathan? I heard what happened. I think you're really brave. I wish I had a son, especially a brave son like you."

I notice he doesn't wait for me to answer his question. I know this kind of man. He says things, but he doesn't mean them. I don't trust him, but I really want to know what the message on the bottom of the scarab says.

"Can you read hieroglyphs? I found this scarab in the tomb. Can you read it for me?" He is immediately interested. I can tell he likes teaching.

"Sure, let's see. 'netr netr hab war sidim ikr sida neb sida hin no ra.' Translated, it means something like, 'May the gods send strong, excellent travel to the owner. May he travel with Ra.' That's a pretty powerful message."

"Thank you, sir." I'm surprised he's so honest with me. Maybe it is powerful and that's why Dad didn't tell me.

Dr. Gorman gets up and starts to leave with my scarab. I'm sure I can't trust him.

"Please give the scarab back," I say. He keeps walking towards the exit. I yell, "Give it back! GIVE IT BACK!" I can't reach it. I try to stand, but it hurts. I can't go after him.

The light in my tent changes and Dr. Gorman looks scared. I think he sees something. His face is screwed up like he's scared. He backs away and out of my tent.

People have come over and are looking at him. They heard me yelling. Then Dad comes in and asks, "What's the matter, son?" I didn't even know he was back from the hospital.

All the people gathering outside have forced Gorman back into my tent. "You thought I would keep your beetle? Sorry."

I don't think he's sorry.

"Your boy thought I was going to keep his scarab. I was just reading the bottom for him."

Dad takes hold of his upper arm and pulls him toward him. "Gorman, you have a reputation for stealing artefacts for your own collection. The university has asked me to ensure you are kept honest." Dad takes my scarab and gives it back to me.

"That's a load of crap!"

"I have my eye on you. Leave my son alone!" Dad demands.

"Don't threaten me, Johnsten. I have my own resources!"

A change comes over Dr. Gorman's face. I think Dr. Gorman sees something else. He's afraid of something again. I wonder if he can see Khepri or sense His power or something.

Then I see it; a smoky cloud, like in the tomb. The jackal-god I saw arguing with Khepri appears behind Dr. Gorman. Set, Khepri called him. He's staring at me. Set opens his mouth and his teeth gnash like he's biting the air. Dad doesn't notice and takes Dr. Gorman out of my tent.

I look up. Khepri is there. He's probably been there the whole time; I just couldn't see him. "Your braveness is wondrous," he says. He slowly leaves, but now I have a feeling he'll always be with me.

"Dad, do I have to give the scarab to the museum?"

"Oh no, Jonathan. The locals sell those scarabs to every tourist."

It gets hot in the afternoon, even in the winter in Egypt. I'm in my tent reading and dozing a bit when someone comes by again.

"Knock, knock," a voice says. I limp to the flap and open it. Dr. Gorman. I stumble back, my hand on my crutch. He certainly is very persistent. (It's a new word I learned.)

"Sorry if I scared you earlier. Here's a treat to make up for it." He holds out a bag of candy. I sense something is wrong, but I would like some candy. I start to reach, but as I realize I shouldn't, he grabs me and carries me under his arm. I yell, but there is no one close. He carries me to the parking lot. I kick and scream and desperately wish I were more than ten. I feel helpless. I'm screaming, "Help! Help me!"

A hand comes over my mouth. I bite it.

"You bloody kid!" Gorman yells and slams me against his car. My breath is knocked out of me and I feel so helpless; he's so much bigger than me.

Then everything stops. He drops me. I look up and see big Abdoullah with his arm under Gorman's neck.

"I suggest you get in the car and never come back or you will have a face to charge of kidnapping."

Abdoullah might not have his words in the right order, but Gorman is stunned at being caught and forced into his car. His red face shows me how embarrassed he is. He leaves quickly.

"Thanks, Abdoullah. I was so scared when Gorman started shoving me into his car."

As Abdoullah and I walk back—well, I limp—I keep my hand on his arm, and I can faintly see the shape of Khepri in the swirling sand near us.

Dad comes rushing up. "I thought I heard you yell, Jonathan, but when I looked in your tent . . . What happened?"

"It was Dr. Gorman. He tried to kidnap me."

Abdoullah adds, "It's the true, Doctor. He was carrying Jonathan to try and shove him in his car."

"I'm sorry, son. I wasn't here fast enough." I can see Dad cares.

"It was luck happening that I was just at the right place," Abdoullah says.

"That man will never be welcome here again," Dad responds.

A couple of days later, Abdoullah, Mum, and I go to the Luxor Museum. There are some things there my dad found. There are lots of brightly painted coffins and two statues of scribes. One scribe statue is fascinating. It's of an old, wrinkled man. He peers out at me.

I think I see his lips moving. I get as close as I can to the glass in front of the exhibits. I can just hear him whispering, "We will meet again." I look up. Mum didn't hear a thing. Maybe there's something wrong with me.

The statue I like most is a beautiful one of King Thutmose III showing his powerful muscles and his handsome face. He seems to be smiling at me.

Those happy days are soon over. A few days later, Mum and I leave to go home to Vancouver.

Dad will be able to leave when his contract is finished. He says goodbye, gives Mum a kiss, and puts his arm around me.

I go and find Abdoullah. I try to be grown up and shake his hand. He shakes mine and then bends down and hugs me. "Stay very safe, little man," he whispers in my ear.

I don't want to leave him. I guess you can tell by now; Abdoullah is my hero.

CHAPTER ONE
HOME IN VANCOUVER

Today, I'm on my daily run. I run down the street, to the end of the block, turn at the corner, and run back past our house. It's a goddamn mansion with a fancy front made of phony Greek pillars, six of them, holding up a covered porch. There are rad leaded-glass windows on both sides of the porch.

Maybe this sounds ungrateful, but when we had a smaller house, we were in each other's lives more. Dad used to come for a run with me if he was home, but now he's famous, always doing research in his office for his next book about Egypt. He really isn't out of shape; he goes to a local gym sometimes. He even has his hair and his eyesight. Not bad for forty-something.

I love going into his office. He has this great painting on papyrus of King Thutmose III on his war chariot. On his desk is this fabulous silver statue of Horus, the hawk, with gold outlines down his wings and above his eyes.

I power up on my stride. "Hunh, hunh, hunh," I breathe as I run down our street and look at the view: stately mansions, perfect lawns, and properly placed trees and flower beds.

Yeah, I know I sound jaded (sorry; I like words). I've worked hard at school, graduating early. I try to help out around the house by cutting the lawn or bringing in the groceries for Mum. It should count for something. I wish Dad would say he thinks I'm great or talk to me more about his projects. He knows I'm interested! I feel like he doesn't really care.

Suddenly—shit—I'm shocked out of my thoughts! "Watch where the hell you're—" I try to yell, but I'm totally stunned and can't even finish my sentence. This car comes right at me, right up on the sidewalk. Screaming, I jump from the street, over the sidewalk, and onto someone's lawn. Then I realize, *he* pushed me to safety. Khepri-Ra is with me, my protector. I didn't even see him. The car drives on up the street and slows, does a U-ey, then comes back towards me. There's a face in the window—a face full of anger, full of hate. My heart is racing and I'm sweating. Not from running, from fear. I know that face. Dr. Gorman. Unforgettable. Suddenly, I remember when he tried to kidnap me. And in the back seat, is that a dog?

I'm about to shout again, but the car swings into our driveway! What's up with that? My thoughts are all mixed up.

I wonder what the hell just happened. I automatically run for a few more seconds and run to the front door. I'd better find out what's going on.

When I open the front door, Rex, my golden retriever, runs to meet me. I give him a pat and say, "Good boy."

I hear muffled shouting; I run down the hall to Dad's office and peer in to make sure he's all right. I'm afraid crazy Gorman will do something to Dad.

Dad is standing behind his desk and there's Gorman, his face red with anger, yelling at him. I really hate that man. It's like a bad play: Gorman is shaking his fist in Dad's face.

"I want you to tell me!"

"Gorman!" Dad says. "Calm down." He puts his hand out but Gorman knocks it away.

"I'm still Dr. Gorman. I'm just not a professor, thanks to you." He steps back.

"You want me to tell you why you lost your job? You're a thief and a fraud. You blamed me for writing that paper for the university. Well, they asked me to. Then you refused to return artefacts that belonged to the university. When the RCMP raided your house to collect them, they found more items belonging to the university and the Egyptian government that they didn't even know you had stolen."

Gorman gets closer to Dad. My muscles tighten and I'm shaking.

"It's all lies!" Gorman screams. "You never gave me credit when I worked with you. It was all you, you, YOU! Now, you've got the scarab." He looks like he's going to reach out and strike my father, but he doesn't.

"You proved their allegations yourself! You've no one else to blame! And listen, it's Jonathan's scarab, not mine. You know that. Now get out of my house!"

I don't know why Dad said "listen;" Gorman isn't listening.

I expect Gorman to pull out a gun, but instead, he picks up the heavy silver Horus from Dad's desk and goes to hit my father. I step forward and grab his arm, surprising him. I hold his arm while Dad grabs Horus.

There is movement in the window. Set, the jackal headed, God of Storms and Chaos, is staring at me. I'm distracted. Gorman shoves me hard and I stumble backwards.

"What the hell?" I yell as I try to keep my balance. Where is Khepri-Ra? I need to rub the scarab, but first, I must dial 911. I pull out my phone, but Gorman knocks it out of my hand and runs right out the front door.

"Thanks, son. He's one crazy guy," Dad says as I pick up my phone.

"I know. He tried to run me down with his car when I was out for my run."

I feel confident, but I confess all this crazy stuff has me wondering if I can cope.

"Are you all right?" Every once in a while, Dad surprises me.

"Yeah. I'm all right. Should we call the cops?" My mind keeps running, *I would like some protection. I think Dad has a gun somewhere. Maybe if Abdoullah were here.*

"I need to thank you for running into my office.," Dad says.

"The police," I repeat.

"I think the guy hates me enough. He sure has a lot of hate," Dad admits. "I wonder if someone actually screwed him over," he adds. I look back at the window. Now Khepri is there, facing Set. His lips form a smile. I can relax.

"Jonathan, listen. I know this might not be the best time to tell you, but the Egyptian government has asked me to head up a dig. They want new discoveries to attract tourists. I must go. It will be for the season, four months."

"I expect you to be responsible for things here. Help your mother. You know she's not well right now. She puts up a front that everything is fine, but it's not. You're only focused on yourself, keeping fit and having fun. Well, that needs to change. Your mother needs you!"

I have been so self-centred. I hadn't even noticed she was sick. I realize this is our man-to-man talk. Well, I guess I'll have to step up.

It appears Dad now values me. He's so confusing. First, I'm a kid who can't do anything. Now, I'm an adult who is expected to step up. I'll show him. I can cope. Even better than that.

He sniffs. "My god, Jonathan, Go take a shower!"

I raise my arm. He is right again. I take a minute to recover from him shouting, not from the smell. I'm startled. This entire day has been weird so far. Too many weird things are happening in my life.

As I leave, I look to my right. There in the window is the jackal with bared teeth. I look up at the figures my dad has on top of the bookshelf. There is Set, the God of Storms and Violence. Could this be Set—in ancient Egyptian, Suetekh—the jackal-headed god? At the window? In Gorman's car? How weird is that?

I look around for Rex. He's usually following me. I open the back door to see if he's outside.

"There you are." I attempt to pat his head. He turns to face me and bares his teeth. "What's the matter, boy?" He just keeps growling. "What's wrong, Rex?" I say, my fear growing. I fear the worst.

I look around. There is Gorman, and behind him Set, the muscular, jackal-headed God of Evil.

"Why have you returned, Gorman?" I yell. What is he planning to do? I try not to seem scared.

An ominous cloud covers the sky.

"Have you heard of the expression, 'selling your soul to the Devil?'" Gorman smiles. "Well, for special power, the power of all the evil gods of Egypt, I have done just that!" He laughs a hollow laugh.

Set raises his WAS sceptre. Lightning flashes around us.

All at once, Set is surrounded by his partners. I recognize them from a YouTube video called "Fierce Gods of Egypt." Ammit, the Destroyer, his crocodile head snapping; Apep, Spirit of Evil and Destruction, his red and gold snake body rearing up; and finally, I recognize Shezmu, God of Execution and Slaughter, his lion face smiling while his fangs drip blood.

I run backwards, but it doesn't matter; they appear right in front of me. Fuck. I'm shaking. I feel like I have a fever. Sweat is dripping from my forehead. I brush it away with my hand.

'Come on, Jono, get a grip,' I say to myself.

"It was so easy to put a spell on your puppy," Gorman taunts me.

Maybe I am going crazy! I'm not sure what to do. I feel powerless, like when I was stuck in that little room in the tomb. In an instant, Set's dark cloud—and with it his companions—vanishes.

The sun breaks through. Khepri-Ra, the rising sun. I hear a whisper, "I am here."

I wish he had stood up to Set. *'Maybe he did? Set did just vanish,'* I say to myself.

I head up to take that shower. I strip down and admire my body in the mirror. I've been working on my arms and shoulders. It seems to me like I'm in three worlds. Mine, Dad's, and Gorman and the Gods'.

Once dressed, I stick my head in my father's office. "Dad, can you check out Rex, please? He's acting weird. And Dad . . . are the gods of ancient Egypt still powerful?"

Maybe an Egyptologist knows something about these strange occurrences. Dad stops what he's doing and looks at me. He has transformed from Dad to Doctor Johnsten.

"Where did that come from?" He keeps looking straight at me.

"Well, I'm not sure, just stuff." I mumble.

"You can talk about it. I'm ready to listen. I think your trip to Egypt really affected you."

"Yes, it did," I reluctantly answer.

"Did you experience something in that tomb in Saqqara?"

"Yes, I, ah, wasn't sure how to, ah . . . Sorry I didn't tell you, but when I was cleaning the dirt off the scarab, this smoke or cloud filled my space in the tomb. I saw Khepri."

"I think you were hallucinating. Scared. Stuck in a small space. You found the scarab and the god has a scarab head. And the limestone block, the pain—it all contributed. Thinking like that isn't healthy, Jonathan."

"And Set?" I asked, hoping Dad would start helping.

"You've seen Set?" I can see he thinks I'm crazy.

"You don't believe me." I turn to leave; I'm not going to argue. I have no proof.

"Jonathan, come back, I want to believe you."

I ignore him. He wants to believe me, but he still thinks I'm hallucinating. That word. His voice. "Hallucinating" is echoing in my mind.

I go out the front and around the back, but I don't see Rex. I call. No answer. I make a trip to the beach since he loves running up and down our beachfront. No Rex. Then I try running around my usual route and back. No Rex.

Once inside, I go to my computer and post him missing on a couple of sites. He hasn't been gone long but I'm worried about what Gorman might have done to him.

Later, when we sit down together for dinner, no one says anything. No one asks about Rex. My mother fills the silence by saying, "It's so nice we're all sitting down together."

It's silent for another minute before I say, "Sorry, Dad, for coming into your inner sanctum smelling like a jock." He almost smiles. I try again. "I'm really interested in the research you're doing."

"It's groundbreaking," he finally says. He's always happy to talk about his work. "I'm needed to find a pharaoh's name in the ruins of her temple. I did some of the work, examining the ushabtis and the broken canopic chest I was able to bring home, but I'm sure if I go, I can get more evidence. Her name, Tausret, one of the few women kings."

"So, you'll look for her temple when you're in Egypt?"

"The remains of her temple. Yes, that's the plan. There's not much of it left."

"You know, I'd be a great gofer." I keep hoping I can go back. The excitement of finding something is so strong.

He doesn't hear me—or at least pretends not to—and continues. "Tausret. Some authorities write it, 'Twosret.' She was the last pharaoh of the nineteenth dynasty and regent for her son, Si-ptah, but he died after just a short time, and she ruled alone as female pharaoh! I researched her for a book I wrote on that dynasty."

Yes, Dr. Darryl Johnsten, author! I just have to get him talking about his research and he'll chat with me like a colleague. I just love that.

"That's fascinating! I know from studying hieroglyphs that the quail chick hieroglyph could be 'w' or 'u.'"

Dad looks up and smiles. "Very impressive. But you still can't come with me." He smirks. He tricked me with a compliment and a swat—an old trick. It really works.

I decide to change the subject. "Did you check on Rex?" I hoped he had.

"Sorry, forgot."

"Damn you!" I breathe.

"Jonathan!" I guess Mum heard me.

The rejection and his forgetfulness boil over. I stand up. "How could you forget? You know how much Rex . . ."

Mum stands. She looks so disappointed.

I turn and look Dad right in the eye. "Excuse me. How often do I ask for help?"

He looks me in the eye. I won't be stared down. After a moment, I leave the dining room. My mother starts to follow me.

"Let him go, Beth."

I don't go downstairs for breakfast the next morning or when I hear Dad leave for Egypt. Am I behaving like an idiot? Probably. But does he love me? I don't know. I feel stupid, eighteen years old and needing my dad's love.

I go for another walk along the beach where Rex loves to run. I call out his name but get no response. I face the fact that he may be gone, permanently gone, and I feel like I've lost a family member.

Mum goes to bed early, but I need to get out. I'm just brushing my hair and deciding where to go when the doorbell rings.

I head downstairs and open the door to see a long-haired guy standing there. I've never seen him before but he's holding a printout of my lost dog post.

"Do your own a golden retriever?" he asks.

"Did you find him?" I quickly respond without answering him.

"He's in my car. Not in good shape. Been to hell and back!"

I follow the man to his car and see that it is, in fact, Rex. I'm so glad he's back, but it's sad to see him lying there, clearly in distress. His coat is damp and has lost its usual shine. He looks limp, like all the energy has been sucked out of him. I think of Set and realize that may have been what's happened.

I pull out my wallet and reach for several twenties. I'm so grateful this guy has brought Rex home.

"I don't want money," the long-haired guy says. "Just glad to get this poor dog home."

"Thank you, thank you." I mumble. After he leaves, I realize I didn't even get the guy's name.

I carry Rex into the house and sit with him on the chesterfield. Mum comes into the living room a few minutes later.

"Who was that at the door?" She looks at Rex. "Oh, poor Rex, he looks terrible."

"Some guy saw my posts online and brought him home."

I bring his water dish in from the kitchen and try to get him to drink, but he can barely lift his head.

"I don't think he even has the strength to drink," I say.

"Try using a baster and squirting water into his mouth."

"Good idea, Mum."

She goes out to the kitchen and returns with a baster. It works. He swallows and wants more.

"Hey, Rex, what happened to you, boy? What did Set do to my fella?"

"What did you say?" Mother asks, looking quite bewildered and strained.

"Nothing. It's complicated. I've been having strange . . . well, connections with Egypt. I've been helped and threatened."

I pause. I know Dad didn't tell her about Gorman. He doesn't want to worry her, but I don't like keeping things from her. "Dr. Gorman came over the other day while you were sleeping and threatened Dad, Rex, and me. He talked about getting help from Set. I know it sounds weird, but you should try living with it."

"I think I know something about your situation. Before we came home from Egypt all those years ago, a young man named Abdoullah came to me and told me you're special. I told him I knew that, but he said you're more special than normal. He intimated that you had contact with Egypt's ancient gods. He said he knew it sounded strange but said it might explain things that happen to you later in life. So, I am forewarned."

I look Rex over. There are a couple of small burn marks on his side, like he had been zapped with something.

Set's two-pronged sceptre. The WAS! I feel sick. What world am I in? Damn you, Gorman.

The second day, Rex starts to move around again. I get him to drink water out of a bowl twice, though he's not strong enough to stand for very long.

On the third day, he finally eats some dog food. He likes the canned meat I give him. It's not his usual meal, but he deserves a treat. It's so good to see him standing up and looking stronger.

Finally, after four days, he's walking properly again. *What had Gorman and Set done to Rex? What could they do to me? I know, I'm rambling.*

I take him for a longer walk now that he's feeling better, but I keep a close eye on my surroundings. I'm sure Gorman's hate and the power of Set and His cohorts could still wreak havoc on Mum, Rex, and me.

Eventually, I decide I need to get out and forget about this craziness for a while! I go to a downtown pub, MacMillan's. They are popular because they don't check for I. D. I sit and have a beer. I can't believe it, but a few tables away, I see an old friend. He had moved to Ontario, but we've been friends since we were kids and kept in touch online.

"Hey, Nathan, ol' buddy. I should have known I'd find you in a bar."

"I just moved back. High five. Good to see you, Jono. Yeah, moved back this week. Moving is not my idea of a good time, so I skipped out for a beer. Good to be back in God's country. What've you been up to?"

No one but Nathan calls me Jono. It was good to hear it again. I give a boring answer. "Graduated, trying to work out four times a week, hope to buy a car. Not a whole lot."

We chat, then I see he's fascinated by something. "See that chick at the bar? Tight blue t-shirt. I think she's hot."

I recognize that look. "Why don't you try your luck? Hunk like you, you're swole. Should have her beggin' for it." He laughs at my stupid joke.

"I'm sick of rejection. Chicks say, 'You guys are all the same. Just want some fun and then run.'"

"Prove her wrong. Show you're a nice guy who will respect her. Might be a welcome change."

I watch Nathan walk over and flip his blond hair back. It's funny that he still does that. When I was about eight, I was so mad because Nathan's dad was taking him to the circus and my dad was in Egypt—but his dad was nice and took me too. I smile, remembering us laughing at the clown act and Nathan flipping his hair back.

Nathan's a nice guy; he deserves to have a girl who will appreciate him. I have another swig of beer then look up, stunned. WTF? Gorman is standing at the bar, staring at me. I came here to escape!

I sit here with my beer, trying to focus on Nathan chatting up the cute girl. He's right, that t-shirt is tight. As much as I try to distract myself, I'm very uncomfortable with Gorman being here. Well, more than uncomfortable. Damn irritated. I'm going to try the old count-to-ten-and-keep-your-cool technique.

I look around the bar and then back, and Gorman is still staring at me. I'm going to tell him off!

"Okay, Dr. Gorman, are you gonna stare at me all night? Stop stalking me!"

"Where's your father? Still doesn't have time for his kid?"

I tense up. I want to sock this phony. I shout at him, "Leave my dad out of this." He knows my sore spot and pokes it.

Out of the corner of my eye, I see this tough guy—the cute girl's boyfriend, presumably—push Nathan. I hear him yell, "Hey, dude, that's my chick!"

"Maybe she'd like a change!" Nathan responds.

The tough guy counters, "Maybe you'd like some of this!" He swings and Nathan ducks.

I don't see Gorman sneaking around behind me, but suddenly, he grabs my shirt and yanks it up tight.

"Bring it on, old man," I yell, challenging him.

"Give me that scarab. I want it and if I don't get it, I'm going to hurt your mother and make your dad wish he had never left you. I'm going to use the power I have to make your dog crazy again."

I'm furious that this lowlife is threatening my family. I'm not as heavy as he is, but I'm fast. I grab his wrist, give him a knee to the groin, turn him around, and smack his back hard against the bar.

"I love my dog, you fuckwit!"

He's done. I let go and he falls to the floor.

I look over at Nathan. He's in a three-against-one. He really needs help so I run over and punch the tough guy several times. Two other guys—friends of the tough guy, I guess—are punching Nathan. I get in several punches, but I get as good as I give. Still, it's my first fist fight ever and I'm winning!

Now, Nathan is fighting with yet another guy. It gets wild and a bunch of bystanders join in!

Gorman struggles to his feet, staggers over to me with a bottle. He aims the bottle at my head. I duck and the bottle smashes on the floor.

The bartender has had enough of this. He yells, "I'm callin' the police!"

Gorman yells back, "Good idea!"

I hope they nail Gorman.

The guys who started this mess keep on fighting. Nathan and I are not going to get out of this easily.

The police arrive minutes later as Nathan and I are standing over the two guys that started it all. Most guys have ducked out and there's no sign of Gorman. Go figure.

The bartender informs the officers, "These two guys," he points at Nathan and me, "started it."

I yell out, "No friggin' way. This guy—"

But the officer cuts me off, "Just shut up." The two officers handcuff me and Nathan.

"I was just helping a friend," I say.

Nathan tries to explain. "Look, sir, I was just chatting with this—"

"Save it for the judge," the officer responds. Being arrested makes me feel really small. Dumb. I'm not a lawbreaker.

As we wait at the booking desk in the police station, I realize I've been a jerk. I encouraged Nathan and I jumped in and escalated the thing.

They fingerprint us as though we've committed some huge crime. It was just a bar fight.

"Look, my father has a lawyer who works for his company. I'm phoning him. I don't care how stupid it makes me look," Nathan yells over the noise of the drunks and prostitutes and all the crazies who are protesting they are innocent. He is right. I can't see another way out.

I think I see the jackal in the crowd of people at the booking desk, but when I double-check, he's vanished. I'm definitely going crazy.

A woman with too much makeup comes on to me, saying, "Say, fella, you wouldn't have fifty bucks would ya? I'll make it worthwhile later."

"Sorry, lady," I reply. "I've got problems of my own." She's no lady and I'm not sorry. Why do we say these things?

I hold up the handcuffs. "Besides, my hands are tied."

"Everybody's a comic." She smirks and leaves.

They stick us in a cell where there's just enough room for me to pace back and forth.

"Will you fuckin' sit down? You're making me crazy," Nathan states firmly.

"I feel sick about this. I'm the one who prodded you, Nathan. And Gorman. He helped get it going."

"Who?"

"A guy who used to work with my dad. Dr. Gorman. Met him in Egypt. Wants this scarab I found. Threatened me and my folks."

"Slow down. This guy threatened you? What's a scarab?" Nathan shouts. I've never seen him get so mad. He's under too much stress and I'm not helping by listing all these crazy things he knows nothing about.

We're in a desperate situation here and I need to do something. I know it will freak Nathan out, but I trust him. I take the scarab from my pocket and rub it. It glows brightly.

"Holy fuck!" Nathan blurts, startled. I realize I've haven't said anything about my secret Sacred Scarab glowing. "What's going on?" he asks, gazing at the glowing beetle.

"I know it's a cliché, but it's a long story. Later, man."

I'm trying to figure out what Khepri can do to help us in jail, but he doesn't appear.

Finally, after what feels like an eternity, the lawyer comes and takes a long look at us. She asks a few questions and I only lie a bit when I say I'm going to university in the fall. I thought it would sound better, even though I want to shove the idea.

We're very relieved when she says we can go home with a court date. I think that might be the end of our friendship, but Nathan is a true friend. He's sticking by me. I really don't deserve him.

The sun is coming up as we leave the police station, and my mother is waiting for me. I try to get ready to grovel.

"How did you know I was here?" I ask.

"Nathan's mother. Jonathan, you didn't think, did you? This is so like you, 'Mr. Impetuous!' Things don't just happen, you know. You make a decision. Look at your face."

I look in the mirror. She's right, I look like a thug. Blue and purple are my favourite colours, though.

Right there in the car, I realize I can't defend myself. She's right. I behaved like a real loser.

We're partway home when Mum starts moaning, holding her stomach. She has to stop the car.

"Are you all right?" I ask. "What can I do?" It's so strange to see a parent get sick. It's like you're in a new world where the roles are reversed; the person who was always there for you now needs you to be there for them.

"Just give me a minute; I'll be okay in a minute."

I realize it will be more than a minute. She is really in pain. "Should I drive?"

"Yes, you drive," she says very quietly. Now I'm sure she's not well. I drive slowly, taking side streets.

When we get home, I say, "Let me help you," and Mum takes my arm. I help her up the steps and into the house, take her shoes off, and get her onto the bed. Then I call the doctor. Fortunately, I get through to the doctor after telling the nurse it's about my mum, Beth Johnsten.

"What is this about?" I ask Dr. Baldwin when he picks up the phone.

The doctor surprises me. "I've been expecting this. She has some prescription medication with her. Give her two tablets. I'll drop over after I see my last patient, about 5:45."

A house call! She must be sick. How could I have been so blind? Never even noticed. Talk about self-centred. *I must focus on Mum,* I tell myself.

When Dr. Baldwin comes, as promised, I take him into Mum. Then I leave but wait for news in the hall.

I text Nathan and tell him what's going on. We were going to meet up, but that isn't going to happen now.

I sit on a chair in the hall until Dr. Baldwin comes out from the bedroom.

"What can I do, Doctor? I mean, is there something I can do? What's wrong with her?"

Dr. Baldwin sighs. "It's Crohn's Disease. Be here. Your mother will have good days and bad days. With this disease, stress doesn't help. I've prescribed metronidazole. She has about a week's worth. There's a repeat on the prescription. She may get ill soon, but she may be fine for a good long time. See if you can get her to take a walk. Just start with a very short one. I mean unbelievably short. She's weak. Check in with her constantly to see if she's tired. You'll need patience."

I see the doctor out. "Thanks so much for coming, Doctor."

I sit down for a few minutes. *Stress doesn't help.* The doctor's words echo in my mind. I can't help but feel this is my fault. And I need patience? Where am I going to get that from? I feel incapable. A better word is inept. Yeah, inept.

I go into her bedroom but she's already asleep. I put a blanket over her.

The next day, Mum and I go out for a walk. She hangs on my arm like I'm the only thing that matters. We only make it down the driveway and back, but we walked! It's a major event for her. We keep up with a walk a day. We make it half a block and back, then eventually, we walk a whole block and back.

We're having our regular cup of tea one afternoon when Mum says, "Jonathan, I know you've never been in trouble before." Looking very serious, she asks, "What happened at MacMillan's Pub?"

I was glad she had given me time to process the whole debacle, (sorry for the vocab again) so I wasn't feeling defensive. "It all started with Dr. Gorman coming to the house, and then being at the pub the next week," I reply. "He was making smart remarks. He threatened to hurt you, Dad, and Rex. I lost it. I should have walked away, but I didn't."

"And what else happened?"

I had to tell all of it. "Nathan was chatting up a girl and her boyfriend didn't like it so he started a fight. Then Nathan was surrounded by a group of the guy's friends, three of them on Nathan, punching him. So I got involved."

"Did you ask the bartender to stop it? Jonathan, did you think about what else could have been done? Police?"

"No, I didn't stop and think," I say. I guess my mother knows me.

***

With Halloween just about a month away, our walks start to get a bit more exciting as the neighbours put up decorations. We're walking our same route to the end of the block and back, admiring the newly added ghosts, goblins, and spiderwebs, when I see a tree covered with plastic body parts dangling from the branches. I chuckle to myself as we pass it.

"What? What is it?" Mum asks.

"That tree with all those body parts. It reminds me of when I was young and Dad was away, and you would tell me the myths of Egypt." I see a smile spread on her face. I know these are happy memories for her too. "The tree looks just like one of my favourites, the story of Set and his brother Osiris, the king. I remember being so upset the first time you told me Set killed Osiris and chopped up his body. But you told me, 'Wait, wait! It gets better!'"

We laugh together, my mother's laugh loud and long. She's getting stronger. I'm so relieved.

"Well, it did get better, right?" Mum answers. "Osiris' wife Isis and sister Nephthys collected all the pieces and put them back together, but—"

"His penis was missing!" I blurt out. We roar with laughter once again.

"It didn't end too badly for him though," Mum continues once we've calmed down. "Isis did make him a new penis made of gold. Osiris came back from the dead, and then Horus was born."

"Egyptian mythology and Sex Ed. in one story," I laugh.

Coming home from our walk, we're met by a very bouncy Rex. His coat has its old golden shine back, and his eyes are bright and clear. He's back to his old self. Rex sometimes walks with us and likes to run ahead and then back to me. I've noticed he tries to stay close. He used to stay in the back garden on his own during the evening, but now he comes in the house and curls up at my feet.

It's Vancouver, so it's rarely cold. Mum and I even walk in the rain, with an umbrella, of course. But today, it's raining harder and lightning forks across the sky. As we hurry home, the sky grows dark. There is a loud thunderclap and Mum jumps at the sound. Lightning zaps the umbrella, which fries, and pain grips my hand as the umbrella vibrates. What the hell just happened? We're freaked out! Luckily the umbrella has a wooden handle.

I look up and see Set standing in front of us. I'm stunned. I throw the smoking umbrella at him and he vanishes into the rain, laughing.

I'm just standing there, soaking wet.

"Jonathan, was that a man or a jackal?" Mum breathes.

She could see him, too. I'm not hallucinating. A cloud of purple surrounds us. Khepri is barely visible. "I'm here, Jonathan. I'm here."

He's watching out for me. Mum hears him too. She looks at me. "It's true," she says.

We walk home in silence, then try to make sense of what happened. As we sit drinking hot chocolate, Mum says, "Your father said he thought something happened to you in Egypt. He told me about your scarab. We agreed not to mention it unless you wanted to discuss it. Well, maybe this is the time. It seems we can't escape it."

I realize I should say something about the whole situation. "I feel weird about it. It's so unbelievable."

"Just start. I'll ask questions if I think you're losing your mind." She smiles and I relax. I know she'll listen.

So I begin, "You know some of what happened already. I showed you the scarab. If you've seen a picture of the god Khepri, you know he has a beetle-face. When I was cleaning the scarab in the tomb at Saqqara—well, rubbing it—Khepri appeared in the tomb. He promised to be my protector but Set appeared. He wanted to add me to his collection of young boys, but Khepri and Ra sent him packing, sort of. Did you see Khepri today?"

"No, sorry, but I heard him. I heard him say, 'I am here.' Mum takes a moment. She is taking in the change in my world. Well, it's her world now too. Then she returns to her situation.

Mum is back to being business-like. "Jonathan, your father wants some books sent. Can you get them to him sometime this weekend? I have to work; I must finish the paperwork on a couple of cases before I take sick leave. Find the books in his office. Here is the key. You should get them ready to ship as soon as possible. Here's his list and the address to ship them to in Egypt."

Once Mum is upstairs, I phone Aunt Peggy, Mum's sister, and tell her Mum's not well. It takes twenty minutes to answer all her questions. I don't tell Mum, but Peggy says she's coming for a visit.

Then I text Nathan. He's up for anything to kill a couple of hours. He arrives in the time it takes me to go down to the basement, rummage through a pile of stuff to find two sturdy cardboard boxes and bring them up to the office. I grab the list and the money Mum left for shipping, making sure not to forget the tape and labels. Right on cue, Nathan rings the doorbell.

"Dad's office is down the hall on the left." I usher Nathan in. He's surprised. The office is astounding. He is staring at the large papyrus painting.

"That's King Thutmose III wearing the blue war crown. Those bearded guys under his chariot and horse are his conquered enemies."

Nathan stares at the painting, then looks towards the very top shelf of the bookcase containing statues of gods. The second shelf holds statues of pharaohs.

I point the gods out. "Osiris, the Green God of Fertility and the Dead; Horus, the falcon-headed one, is his son and the God of Power and Healing; there's Isis and her sister, Nephthys. The two of them assembled the pieces of Osiris' body when his brother, Set, the God of Storms and Violence, chopped him up. That's Set there with the jackal head. Then there's Thoth, with the ibis head, the God of Knowledge; Sobek, the crocodile god, whose sweat and tears created the Nile and other rivers; and Shezmu, the lion-headed God of Murder."

I try really hard not to sound like a fuckin' know-it-all.

"You know a lot about this." Nathan says as he stares at the statues. I guess it was okay; he just liked the info. "Is this all of them, lined up along this shelf?"

"Oh no, there are a lot more than these seven."

"These make a pretty impressive collection, all lined up. And all these books on ancient Egypt. Your father is hooked!" Nathan blurts.

"It's his job. We don't have to pack them all. Just the ones on this list."

"It would be so cool to go to the museum in Egypt."

"Nathan, *the* museum?" I respond with a smirk. "There's lots."

"How many?" Nathan is incredulous.

"Well, there are museums in lots of places: four at least in Cairo and about five more near major historic sites."

"Wow," exclaims Nathan. "I mean, I read about the new GEM, the Grand Egyptian Museum, at Giza. But all these?"

"Not to mention all the collections of Egyptian treasures in museums all over the world."

I feel the scarab in my jeans move. Weird. I put my hand on it to stop it.

"What's the first book on that list?" Nathan asks. Then I notice a statue moving slowly towards the edge of the bookcase. The Set statue moves. Then it comes to the edge, wobbles and falls toward Nathan. He lets out a yell. It seems to happen in slow motion.

Nathan jumps away, shouting, "Get him away from me!" I catch Set just before the statue hits Nathan.

"It's Set," I tell him. "I have no idea what kind of world I've gotten myself into, but it's very strange!"

"It was as if he was aiming right for me." Nathan is looking pale, and I bet he's been shaken by this craziness.

"As I've found out from various meetings with the guy, Set collects cute young boys. Maybe he thinks you're worth adding to his collection." I try to keep a straight face. Nathan looks at me and we both laugh. Underneath the joking, I think, *Set is powerful. He is evil. He is after me, has his eyes set on me, as they say, so why not on Nathan too?*

Slowly, Nathan recovers and laughs at such a crazy idea, sitting back down. He takes Set from me.

"Ya know, Jonathan, I don't know if he's warning us or just doing what he does, cause confusion."

"Right? Seriously! He just fell off the shelf."

Why am I minimizing this? It's not normal, but here's something interesting about having weird things happen to you: you rationalize them. You say, "I must have imagined it. There's no such things as ghosts or living Egyptian gods." *I mean seriously, Jonathan; who would believe you?* Oh my God, now I'm talking to myself!

"Seriously, Nathan, we'll have to keep watch. Speaking of being serious, Nathan, you read the first title from the list, including the author. I'll find the book. The sooner we get this done, the sooner we can get a cold drink and sit on the terrace."

It takes a while, but we finally finish. We're taping up the boxes and slapping labels on them when I say, "I really could use that drink."

Grabbing a bottle of my dad's smoothest Canadian whiskey, Nathan and I head down to the beach at the front of our house. It always amazes me what money can buy. A waterfront home in Vancouver!

"You know, everything has been crazy since Gorman showed up. I don't know what kind of amulet or spell he uses, but first he came in and fought with Dad. Then I started seeing Set, the god from Dad's shelf. That's your fave. I didn't tell you about the lightning striking the umbrella when I was out with Mum getting some exercise. There was Set the jackal, standing on his hind legs, fangs bared!"

"What? Lightning?"

"Yeah, zapped the umbrella to a crisp."

I decide not to tell Nathan about Gorman selling his soul. Too weird. It would take more than friendship for him to think I'm not bonkers.

By now, we're feeling no pain. Thank god for booze. Nathan and I hit the cold Pacific naked as jaybirds and swim out to a buoy. As we're swimming back, the wind picks up. The ocean starts off being choppy, then waves mount. Swimming gets threateningly difficult. In the clouds that move in, I can see the sheen of Set's silver body. The waves smack us up on the beach, but I have otherworldly help climbing out of the waves. I reach back and pull Nathan out. We grab a towel from the boathouse and have a few more swigs.

Khepri stands there on the beach and Nathan sees him. Nathan says nothing; it's like he's frozen. I give him a second or two, then snap my fingers in his face. It's corny, I know, but it works.

"I told you about Set; now you meet Khepri, my protector. Let's get warm."

We race back to the warmth of the house. I wave to our neighbour, who is watching us naked young men in amazement. Thunder rolls.

"Jonathan, you're naked. Where are your parents?" she shouts over the hedge.

"Yep, we are! They aren't home. Want them to call you?"

Nathan and I laugh as we run towards the house.

"Hey, Nathan, I told you I'd explain some weird things going on. Did you see a big guy with a beetle face on the beach?"

"I thought I'd had too much whiskey and salt water."

"I can understand that. Well . . ."

"Whenever you start with 'well,' I know we're moving into weird territory."

"You're right. When I was a kid, I went to Egypt with my parents. I was taken into a tomb to play at being an Egyptologist. It worked. I found, or I was directed to find, a sheet of papyrus."

"Like in your dad's office? And why did you say directed?"

"I'm not sure what that means, but that's what I was told by Khepri. Wrapped up in the papyrus was a scarab, a special stone carved into the shape of a beetle. The one you saw when we were in jail. The scarab is over four thousand years old and when I cleaned the dirt off it, I sort of rubbed it and it glowed. That glow brought a purple mist into the room of the tomb and Khepri appeared." I didn't tell him I had seen him once before when our jeep went off the road.

"Like, this god appeared in a tomb because you rubbed this stone beetle?"

"Do you believe me?" I ask.

"Look, Jonathan. I saw the statue move slowly to the edge of the bookcase and then fall right toward me. I saw the waves pick up and nearly drown me and a big muscle-bound, beetle-faced guy stood in front of me on the beach. So, look, I would believe anything."

"This beetle-faced guy is the god Khepri; sometimes he teams up with the Sun God Ra. Because I found this scarab, and it is sacred, I made a promise to guard it. In return, Khepri has stated he is my protector." I pause. "I think I've said too much."

"That explains a lot, I think." Nathan says with appreciation.

"Nathan, I don't know how to say this. I'm sure you'll think I'm crazy, but whenever something weird happens with Set, the scarab vibrates or moves. I want to do a test, but I don't want to try this alone. Are you game?"

"What do you mean, 'a test?' What could happen?"

"I'm not sure; let's go to my father's office. This might backfire or do something weird. I have no idea how this will play out, but I have to try. I want to find out if I will go somewhere. The hieroglyphs on the bottom promise travel. I must know the power of the sacred scarab."

"So, you're not sure of the power of the scarab? You think, without knowing why, we might travel somewhere, and you are asking me to try and go we don't know where, because you think this scarab has special power?"

"Yes, Nathan, that about sums it up."

"All right, I might be crazy, or maybe I like taking chances, but let's test your theory."

We look at each other and nod, making a silent pact.

"Okay, I've got the scarab; you hold the silver Horus. That will be our contact with ancient Egypt."

"Are you ready?"

"Just do it before I change my mind!"

I rub the Sacred Scarab. It glows.

"Okay, connect."

We grab our free hands.

The light in the room goes black, then flashes blindingly bright. I'm so friggin' scared. My stomach is all knotted up. I feel swirling, like we're moving around and around, going somewhere. I'm dizzy, yet not dizzy.

"Are you all—" I begin to say, but I'm cut off as we land on the ground.

"Well," whispers Nathan, recovering and looking around, "we came—or went—somewhere."

"I feel like I just experienced an out-of-body trip." I say.

"That seems to be what I'm feeling," Nathan replies.

I look around. "I think we're in a tomb. Look, there's the silver Horus in the painting sitting on the table." On the walls are beautiful, recently finished paintings of an important man sitting with ships under his chair. He must have overseen the navy. The paintings on the walls show servants lined up, giving him bread and ducks.

Suddenly, two men enter. They're not very pleased to see us. They're frowning and speaking to each other in what sounds like very annoyed dialogue. One is the same man we see in the painting.

"Bow," I breathe. We both do.

"Who are you?" the man from the painting asks. It surprises me. I can understand him.

"We come from far away. Your tomb is beautiful, but we know this is a sacred place."

"My name is Wahtye, Vizier of Middle Egypt."

I step forward and bow again.

The muscular friend is not having me get any closer. He approaches us brandishing a staff. I really do not want to extend this trip. Who knows what a guy with all those muscles can do?

Wahtye raises his hand and stops him. He says, "I would like to know will my tomb survive?"

"Yes, it was discovered about four thousand years into your future," I tell him.

"These men are evil sorcerers," the bodyguard or whatever he is, says walking towards us with his cudgel raised.

"Nathan," I yell, holding out the scarab. Our hands clutch it and the light in the tomb goes to black, then flashes totally bright. I feel us swirling around and around again. We land with a thump on the carpet in Dad's office.

"I'm stunned," I say.

"That's not even close to covering it!" Nathan replies.

"How do you feel?" I ask.

"Wow, that was dope; we know it works."

"Maybe someday we'll need it!" I say.

It takes a few minutes to recover. My head is still buzzing. We just sit on the carpet.

"You know, Nathan, if anything else happens, I don't know what will keep me sane."

I hear the door open and shut. Mum walks in. "Just sitting on the floor talking?"

"We'd better take that box of books to the post," I respond.

"Last I looked, there were two," Nathan says with a smirk.

"See what I mean? I'm so out of it."

Coming back from the post office, I drop Nathan off. "Oh, by the way, bro, there's no charge for that trip to Egypt," I say as he steps out of the car. Nathan punches me on the shoulder.

I'm feeling a bit on the tired side so go to my room and crash. I'm not really with it when I think I hear the doorbell ring. I hear Mum answer, "Oh hello, Mrs. Grantham."

Now I'm awake.

Our neighbour states, "I didn't call the police, but I thought you should know your son and his friend were running around naked on the beach side of your house, Beth. And they had a bottle of liquor!"

Mrs. Grantham hurries off as the rain pelts down.

"Jonathan? Jonathan!" Mum calls.

I'm faking being asleep and hope to escape what's coming. Next thing I know, she's shaking my shoulder, so I roll over.

"What were you and Nathan doing? Mrs. Grantham is very upset. She nearly called the police. You were naked?"

Mum does that "tsk" thing to show how awful it was.

"I know you and your father had a chat."

I blurt out, "I was really being a jerk, I know. I'm going to focus. Be responsible. It's a promise."

I get dressed, go downstairs, and make coffee. I text Nathan and ask if he wants a cup. He's here right after it drips. He makes himself at home, like he usually does, going to the pantry.

Then the doorbell rings again.

"You answer it, Nathan. I can't take another crazy!"

Nathan opens the door and Aunt Peggy stands on the doorstep. "I'm here to help," She tells Nathan. Her hair is still in curlers. I guess she left in a hurry. Her classic 1973 Chevy Caprice is parked in the drive. She tells me she only drives it twice a week to do the shopping and go to church.

"Glad you came," I say, rescuing Nathan from having to introduce himself.

"Like I said on the phone, Jonathan, I had to. She's my sister!"

"I'm hungry," Nathan says. He heads back to the pantry.

I haven't even shut the front door when Mum comes out of her office. She looks awful; her face is actually white.

"Jonathan, Jonathan, I've just received a terrible email. Your father is missing."

"What do you mean 'missing?'" First, Mum is sick, then the ancient gods are messing with me, and now my dad is missing. My stomach is tight and my heart is pounding. How could Dad go missing when he works with a whole team of people?

"I was working on my computer in my office," Mom continues. "I got this email. I printed it for you. He was working on a site near Luxor. Excavating a temple, I guess. Here, read it." Tears are welling up in her eyes. "He just disappeared!"

"Like the excavation collapsed?" I ask, trying to get more information.

"I know nothing more." She looks helpless. She sits and tears start running down her cheeks. "Darryl, oh Darryl," she mumbles.

Mum cries into a handkerchief. "It's happened!" she says. "I worry about this every time he goes there." Peggy puts her arm around her.

"I'll look after this!" I shout. "I can do it!"

"Jonathan! Just take a minute and think about it. He wouldn't want you dashing off," Mum warns.

Nathan wanders in from the pantry with a cookie in his hand. "I have a brilliant plan!" he says to me. He clearly hasn't read the room. "I think we should . . ." He rattles on about taking a trip to the interior of BC.

"You might be going to Wells Grey Park," I say, interrupting, "but I'm going to Egypt to find my father. Mum just got an email saying he's missing. I'm going to find him."

"Right!" Nathan says, quickly agreeing. "Count me in!"

"Nathan, I'm worried. Egypt is not a peaceful place. They have revolutions. Egyptologists' sites get robbed. God knows what could have happened. It's my Dad who needs my help. I'm going."

Nathan blurts out, "Not without me!"

You can't say I didn't warn him. Maybe I was warning myself.

"What do you think you can do?" Aunt Peggy asks. She sits and starts taking out her curlers. I think she's trying to get rid of nervous energy.

"Well, I can't do anything from here." Again I'm Mr. Impetuous.

"Jonathan, I can't legally stop you," Mum starts. "You're eighteen, but I think you should think about this. You know I worry about your father. I hear all kinds of terrible reports of things happening in Egypt: rioting, stabbing, kidnapping. If you listened to Al Jazeera, you'd know. I refuse to help you with this. I don't want you to go. If something happened to you . . ." She's crying again. This time, it's my fault.

Mom and Aunt Peggy go to sit in the sunroom. I contact the Foreign Affairs Department. I can tell they're not trying to solve this case yet. They have all kinds of situations just like this all over the world, and this just happened.

Aunt Peggy corners me a while later. "Jonathan, you know the doctor told you that your mother should not have any extra stress in her life. What do you think this is doing? Not only will she have to worry about your father, she'll worry even more about you."

I avoid her caution. "I'll check with Foreign Affairs and see what the situation is like in Egypt right now."

Nathan says reassuringly, "We've got this!"

I'm glad to have the support of my buddy, but we need to get our fight charges settled in court or they'll stop us from boarding a plane. Thankfully, our date in court is set for the day after tomorrow. We wait somewhat impatiently until then.

***

Our day in court arrives and our lawyer does all the talking. I can't believe she's talking about us.

"Your Honour, these are clean-cut, normally sane kids, bound for university. These boys have perfect records and have never even skipped church on Sundays." I don't dare look at Nathan when she says this. I haven't been to church in ages, but if it means getting out of this mess, I'll go.

The judge looks at us sitting there in suits and ties, hair perfectly combed, and he believes her.

I can't help staring at the judge. For some reason, he looks like the ancient Egyptian scribe I'd seen in the Luxor Museum with Abdoullah. His face becomes more wrinkled, and his eyes look like they've seen a thousand years of history.

"From what I've read, you are bright young men who have never committed an offence," the judge begins as his face ages and the lights change. Soon, he's surrounded by a golden glow.

"I know you are going to my home country," the judge says.

I look at Nathan. "Is this spooky or what?" I whisper.

Nathan nods. He moves his hands as if saying, "What gives?"

"You will need my help to find the person you seek," the judge continues. He beckons me to approach to the bench.

He holds out an ANKH, an ancient Egyptian sacred cross-like object with a loop at the top. "Here is a key. I want you to take this with you. This key will open the way. Use your intelligence. Be guided by the ancient spirits, your own spirits, and your ingenuity."

I look at the ANKH. It's clearly very old and is made of dark burnished gold with hieroglyphs. The handle is the right size for my grip. I take it, then sort of bow and stumble, dazed, back to my seat.

The light returns to normal. No one, it seems, has heard the judge's ANKH comments except Nathan and me.

My hearing seems to refocus: ". . . something you can learn from this: Use your intelligence; think first before you act; think of others often; and learn, learn from your mistakes. Property worth five hundred dollars was damaged. I sentence you to pay damages and a fine of two hundred and fifty dollars each. Case dismissed." He bangs his gavel, ending our trial.

I look at the judge. He's just a normal older Canadian man. What just happened? I'm sure it's something weird again!

We contact the Canadian government again to find out what the situation is like in Egypt. Foreign Affairs tells me that Dad's situation is under investigation and that both the Canadian and the Egyptian authorities are taking it seriously, *blah blah blah*.

"Sure," I explode as I hang up, "that means nobody is doing anything!"

Looking back, my mother was right. I should have thought about it for a minute, but well, I'm an impetuous guy. So, we quickly organize our trip so we can leave in four days. We have our passports and can get visas for Egypt online. It only takes seventy-two hours to get them certified.

Before we leave, Mum pulls me aside. "Jonathan," she says, "I know you've made your decision, but I'll worry less if you have this." Mum gives me her credit card. She knows I spent all my money on my fine and travel costs already. I thank her but promise myself I'll avoid using it. It's hard saying goodbye to Mum.

"Be careful, Jonathan. Keep in touch. You can't phone me too often. I don't care if you have nothing to say except 'I'm fine.'"

"Love you, Mum."

Finally, we're off to the airport.

We are standing and chatting in line at the terminal. "This is going to be such a long flight. Seven hours to Frankfurt and then another two to Cairo," I moan.

"It'll be worth it. If we have to search all of Egypt."

"Excuse me," a professional-looking man behind us starts talking. I hadn't really noticed him before.

"Excuse me," he says again.

I turn, startled.

"I heard you mention Egypt," the stranger says.

"Yes," I answer, "that's our destination."

"Sight-seeing?" He asks. He's very friendly. I think he's genuine.

"No, unfortunately, we're going to find someone."

"I work in Egypt. I'm going to join a dig in Abousir." he says. It's starting to make sense.

"Oh wow. My father is an Egyptologist."

"Not Dr. Johnsten, by chance? I heard he's missing."

"Yes, how . . ." Another bit of crazy!

"I'm Dr. Wright, an Egyptologist. Egyptologists in Canada, well, you probably know, are a small group; we keep in touch."

"What a coincidence. Well, not really, I guess."

"I'll be in Cairo for a week, then join the team at Abousir. Good luck finding your father. Here is my card with my Cairo information. Call if I can be of any help," Dr. Wright says.

Finally, we board the plane. The wait had seemed so long, but the flight will be longer. The first leg: Vancouver to Calgary.

After a smooth takeoff, the captain comes on the intercom. "We are in for a bit of a bumpy ride," he says. "Please stay in your seats, make sure your trays are in the upright position, and fasten your seatbelts."

Then it begins: A horrible, jostling ride, much worse than any back road I've ever been on. The plane lifts and then falls with a bang. It rolls from side to side and baggage falls out of the overhead bins. Some passengers are sick; the smell does not help those of us who aren't. Then, just as suddenly as it began, it stops. We have smooth flying the rest of the flight. We change planes, then we're on to Frankfurt.

Somewhere over the Atlantic, I need to use the john. As I wash my hands and check my hair, I scream. Standing right behind me in the mirror is Set. His slanted eyes are almost smiling. The God of Storms. The rough ride. You figure it out. Of course, when he appeared, I'm not proud, I screamed like a five-year-old. I never get used to being startled by Set. I'm shaking. I try and relax, to control my racing heart with slow breaths.

I confront him. "What do you want from me?" Set just gnashes his teeth. Not as effective as it was the first time.

Then, Khepri-Ra is behind the God of Chaos, moving him into the shadows. I nod in thanks.

"What the frig," I sorta whisper to Nathan. "Set was staring at me in the mirror in the can!"

"No way," Nathan replies

"Yes, wa—" I start to say.

I mean, that is such a stupid thing to say. If Nathan had thought, he would have said, "That is completely unbelievable." And I would have replied, "Yes, it most definitely is." But then, neither of us have been educated at Oxford.

We make a quick switch to another plane in Frankfurt and then finally we're headed to Cairo. I can hardly sleep or eat. Neither can Nathan. (Well, I ate the steak dinner on board. Not bad.)

The flight attendant on this last leg of our journey is an older woman. I didn't know they had older flight attendants. She has a long hooked nose almost like a beak and close set eyes. She comes down the aisle checking passengers.

When she gets to me, she bends down. "Do not fear, Jonathan," she whispers, "the spirits of Egypt will be with you." Then she turns and leaves. This is so weird. Why would a stewardess bring me a message? Who is the Egyptian messenger of the gods? I think it's Thoth, the inventor of language and writing and therefore the messenger. I feel like the gods are always in my face. I look back up the aisle and see that the two flight attendants serving drinks are young. I give my head a shake.

Our touchdown is perfect.

CHAPTER TWO
SO THIS IS EGYPT!

The hot, thick air of Egypt hits us the moment we're thrust out of the airport terminal. They say it hits you like a wall. It's true, I tell ya.

Before we can say, "I wonder how to get to Luxor," a large, prepossessing man is in our faces. (I like to show off my vocabulary, sorry.)

"Gentlemen, I am Abdoullah." I hug him and laugh. As if I wouldn't remember the man who saved my life! "Your father said if something happened to him . . . ah, and here you are. I didn't almost recognize you, Mister Jonathan. Your father had your picture, so I could see you as a young man. You grew."

"You wouldn't believe how good it is to see you!" For a second, before introducing Nathan, I vividly remember being that frightened boy stuck in a tomb. "Nathan, this man saved my life twice! Abdoullah, this is Nathan, my best friend. He's crazy enough to come help find my father," I tell Abdoullah. "We're going to Luxor."

I realize this is the first time I've said Nathan is my best friend and that he is committed to helping me. Maybe he should just be committed.

The traffic is amazing. Thousands of cars and trucks moving rapidly through the streets and around hundreds of roundabouts. The estimated population, not including tourists, is eleven million people, and all of them are on the streets. The city busses are hilarious. They're jam-packed with people dangerously hanging on and jumping off at their stop. It's unbelievable. In Canada, once the seats and aisles are full, no more people are permitted. Not in Cairo. If you can find something or someone to hang on to, it's fine. I don't know how they collect fares. I haven't seen anyone doing that.

We weave our way through the city, aware of the exhaust and smells of open-air restaurants and shops, and finally arrive at Cairo West Airport

As we get tickets to fly south, Abdoullah asks, "Why did you say I wouldn't believe how good it was to see me?"

I try to explain. "I know you know those crazy idioms in English. We say, 'You wouldn't believe how much I feel about something,' not because you wouldn't believe it, but because it is such an incredible amount that it's difficult to believe it is that much. Does that help?"

Abdoullah looks at me pityingly.

We fly the short distance to Luxor and touch down within an hour. The temperature is about the same as in Cairo, but there's much less pollution. Abdoullah's cousin Hasaan meets us at the airport. Abdoullah introduces us all before we get on our way to Dad's last dig. Hasaan drives like a city taxi driver in Cairo, fast and smooth, and chats with Abdoullah in Arabic at the same speed. I relax and enjoy the ride until I become aware that Hasaan is speaking loudly.

Abdoullah interrupts him. "Look out the back window, please. We are being followed by a red car, yes?"

Sure enough, I can see a red car. Looking carefully, I see Gorman's face, his dark eyes and perfectly trimmed beard visible in the passenger seat. Those black eyes are unforgettable. I thought I could come to Luxor and feel safe, but no! Here he is following me and giving me the jitters.

"Can we get rid of this tail?" I ask Hasaan.

We pick up speed, drive down two side streets and around a traffic circle, and lose him. We breathe a sigh of relief. I don't know what he could do against four men in good shape, but who wants to find out?

We eventually cross the Nile via the Luxor Bridge and head to Medinet Habu, past the mortuary temple of Ramesses the III, to the dig where Tausret's temple once stood. Always the tour guide, Abdoullah tells us, "This is the place the ancient Egyptians thought the first gods were buried. It was called 'Djamet,' mothers and fathers of all the gods."

We arrive at the site and meet Dr. Czerny, the head of my father's excavation. He comes to the car smiling.

"Welcome again, Jonathan. You've grown into a strong-looking young man. And who is this?"

"My best friend, Nathan Grant. He's helping me find Dad."

"A pleasure. Let's go to my tent and get out of the sun."

At the tent, Dr. Czerny explains, "I was working on a dig in Saqqara when I heard Darryl was missing. I just got here an hour ago myself. He's still missing so I decided to stay and see if I could help."

A tall, handsome man enters the tent. "This is Dr. Bernoune, who was working with your father on Tausret's temple. This is Jonathan, Dr. Johnsten's son, and his friend Nathan Grant. And I think you know Abdoullah." We shake hands quickly.

"Please fill us in, Doctor," I say.

"We were working together. Got down to the base of the temple. We were pleased we were making progress on excavating the foundations of the temple. I don't know what happened. Dr. Johnsten was writing up reports in the office tent and I was working with the team of Egyptians we have hired. We were following the foundation on the eastern side of the temple. I went to see him at the end of the day, and he wasn't at his desk. I searched around the camp. Nothing! He'd just disappeared," Dr. Bernoune admits.

"We need more information so we can find my father," I respond. "Can you call a team meeting to see if anyone saw anything at all?"

"Right away. When I didn't see him, I thought he was still catching up on paperwork. Sounds so thoughtless now. I contacted the police as soon as I realized he was missing. They said all the right things, but took no action," Dr. Bernoune confesses.

When the team is assembled in the large mess tent, Dr. Czerny introduces us. "These men are here to find Dr. Johnsten. This is his son, Jonathan. Did anyone see anything before Dr. Johnsten disappeared? Was he talking to someone? Did he get in a vehicle? Did you see him walking out from our camp? Any scrap of information might help."

A lot of shaking heads. No one saw anything. I feel hopeless. We need some sort of clue.

Then a young guy, whose name we later find out is Jabari, gives us a lead. "I saw Dr. Johnsten arguing with some man. Trimmed black beard. I think he wanted to work here. He and two guys went away with Dr. Johnsten in a van, I think maybe dark green. I should have said something, sorry."

I look at Nathan. I recognize Gorman from the description. I'm suddenly angry. Gorman is crazy. He could do anything to my father.

"Do you have surveillance cameras to provide security for this site?" I ask.

"No, we don't," Dr. Bernoune says. "We should, but the equipment hasn't arrived. This is Egypt. You must chase equipment. I'm so focused on my work. I'm sorry, it isn't a priority."

"Where's the nearest police station?" Nathan says. "Let's do this!"

"Just across the bridge in Luxor," Dr. Czerny says helpfully.

"Jabari," I say, "You're with us." I guess I overstepped. I have no right to commandeer him, but I like the guy and he impressed me because he's observant and took responsibility.

We're off; Abdoullah knows where to go. At the police station, we file a missing person report to get help. From the description, a helpful police officer guesses the van was a rental. No one buys a dark-coloured van in Egypt: too hot. There are two rental companies. The first one we try refuses to give us any information. We call the nice police officer and he comes to the rental office. He seizes their records, just like that. Guess whose name is on the forms as the driver?

"Look at this, Nathan. See anything familiar? I guess you must show your driver's license, even in Egypt. Our first stop is lucky, look at the name: Gorman."

They inform us that the van is overdue. They have devices so they don't lose vehicles. In agreement for returning the van, they give us a tracking device to follow the van.

The van has crossed the checkpoint at Suez, so we're off to the north, skirting Cairo to avoid traffic, and into Sinai. Dr. Gorman must have some reason for taking Dad there.

"It's already hot, like I'm sweatin' man," Nathan says.

"Nathan, you really didn't need to tell us that," I laugh. "Suck it up. We're on a mission!"

Then I get a text: "If you want your dad, come to the caves of Wadi Maghareh."

How did Gorman get my phone number? Of course—from Dad. Well, that's good news, I hope. Where is this place he's taken Dad to? I know he has two motives: to hurt Dad and to get the sacred scarab!

I find the Wadi on the map.

It's also called the Valley of Caves, where for thousands of years, Egyptians mined turquoise and copper. I bet Gorman did research there at some point; he must have knowledge of the area.

We take the road along the Red Sea. After driving about fifty kilometres, we see nothing but badlands, not great for growing anything. In the middle of nowhere, we come to a road running east to Wadi Magareh. Talk about out of the way. Anywhere I've been, there's always a gas station on the corner, at the very least. Here, there's just a signpost.

Several kilometres farther into Sinai we come to some impressive cliffs.

Abdoullah states, "These high cliffs have been known for thousands of years because turquoise was mined here."

"All right, Abdoullah, since you were in the Egyptian army and based here in Sinai, what's the plan?" I say. I think it's time to organize this team.

"We need to be able to do the ambush of these guys. When I was here as a young man, we found a temple that a king had built in front of his mine. I am putting the bet that Dr. Gorman knows of this temple and that is why he has come back to this out of the ways place." Abdoullah says, remembering his past.

"Anyone think Gorman has some men with him?" Nathan asks.

We all do. He usually does. "Jabari, you said Gorman had two goons with him when he grabbed Dad?" I ask.

He nods.

"Jabari and I noticed the tracks of a couple of vehicles on the dirt road after we turned off the pavement," Abdoullah explains.

"Now you tell us!" I say with a grin, "I think it's wise if we camp here for the night. We have sleeping bags. Tomorrow, we can ambush them at first light."

We find a sheltered gully and pitch a tent a suitable distance from Gorman's turquoise cave. It's a beautiful night with thousands of stars. We light a small fire to boil water for tea.

"This little valley was formed by water. I just hope it doesn't rain and wash us out," I say.

"Have you lost it, Johnsten?" Nathan responds. "When do you think it last rained here?"

"Thanks, Nathan."

I go for a little stroll alone. As I sit looking up at the sky, I remember Mum quoting from a book she was reading about Sinai. Mum mentioned it several times, and I wrote the quote in my phone's notebook, but I don't remember who wrote it:

"Wander but a few paces from the camp and listen in the solitude to the low, melancholy sigh of the night wind, which sweeps the light surface of the sand, drifting it against the canvas wall of the tent. That breeze, laden with the voice of ages that traverses the desert, speaks to you as do the thousand stars."

The quiet stillness of Sinai, the bright starlit sky, and the slight wind is a reminder to me the world can have its perfect moments.

I eventually find the comfort of my sleeping bag.

As the sun is lightening the sky, Abdoullah wakes us and we drink warm tea.

I have a plan already percolating. Maybe my mind works in my sleep. I sometimes wake with great ideas and wonder how I got them. Sometimes they're crazy. Fortunately, this is not one of those times.

"Okay, let's get organized. Any thoughts?" I say to encourage the group.

***

"I think I saw a couple of gullies. We know this is the right one because of the tracker."

Abdoullah says, "I am thinking you could drive us closer to the next gully so we would just have to go over the ridge between the two and that would be the easiest way to make the ambush to these guys."

"That would get us behind them, right?" Nathan adds.

"Great idea. Let's do this!"

I drive to the next valley where Abdoullah, Nathan, and Jabari get out of the jeep.

"I'll drive up to where Gorman and his guys are as if I came alone," I explain. "I'll carry on a chat, try to see Dad, and say I have hidden the scarab. There's a gun in my backpack."

"Where did you get a gun?" Nathan asks.

"Dr. Bernoune gave it to me as soon as he heard we were coming to Sinai. He thinks it's wild over here. He made me promise to bring it back to him. Because Dr. Czerny recommended us, Dr. Bernoune made me promise to work on a dig with him in exchange for the gun. The promise includes you too, Nathan."

"Sounds good," Nathan says getting the gun out. I expected him to respond with, "You had no right to make a promise without asking me," but he didn't.

I drive myself up the other valley and stop at the remains of the temple. There's not much left of it, just several columns on a level slab floor. There are some carvings on the rock walls, but I'm not close enough to read them.

I rev the engine and soon Gorman appears, supported by a young man pointing a gun at me.

"Hello, Doctor," I say. "And you must be Dr. Gorman's son. I can see the resemblance." He has the same dark eyes. "Is my dad all right?" I ask.

"No small talk," Dr. Gorman states with a smirk on his sunburned face. "This is my son, Richard, or Rick, but he's no Dick." He laughs at his own attempt at humour.

"Humour at gunpoint?" I say with a smirk.

Rick goes to bring Dad out of the cave. I'm intrigued by the carvings on the rock walls of the valley leading up to the cave. They're large ancient images of kings and hieroglyphs, beautifully carved and preserved.

"I imagine you've done a study of these hieroglyphs, Doctor?"

"Yes, quite interesting. My research proved Hebrew slaves worked these mines."

"I would really appreciate a quick look now that I'm here."

Gorman says, "Of course."

I walk closer to the cave entrance and look. There is a large classic image of the king raising his club over the head of a captive.

"Were you able to conclude who this king is, Doctor?"

"I could date him as Middle Kingdom. Unfortunately, there are no cartouches included on these walls, but we have records of the kings that sent expeditions to Sinai for turquoise and copper. They called the mines the Turquoise Terraces. New Kingdom kings made sure they placed their cartouche on their inscriptions. They were more aware of leaving their mark."

Just like Dad. Get him talking about his favourite topic and he's off.

Rick brings Dad out of the cave. He's looking tired and is probably hungry and dehydrated. I never thought I'd be the one worrying about him. I can tell by his smile that he's glad to see me. I'm relieved to see him too.

"Are you all right?" I yell. I want to run to him, but Gorman demands, "Stay where you are and give me the scarab and the papyrus it was wrapped in."

"You didn't ask for the papyrus. It's in Canada." I hadn't counted on that curve. But there was something that niggled at me. Did the papyrus say something that Gorman hadn't translated for me eight years ago?

"Well, Jonathan, you'll have to send for it," Gorman demands.

Rick moves to return Dad to the cave. In a flash, Abdoullah—stripped to shorts—Nathan, and Jabari jump down from the ridge and take Gorman and his son down.

"You really need to get better at this, Gorman," I gloat.

I should get better myself. Not so cocky, not so impetuous! Two men rush out of the cave with automatic rifles. They take our gun and we're done! I guess I should be glad they didn't shoot.

"Hand over the scarab, Johnsten!"

"You'll have to search for it."

One of his men searches the jeep. "Nothin' here, boss."

Rick walks over and takes great pleasure in patting me down, enjoying any pain or embarrassment he can cause.

"He's got nothin,' Dad," Rick laughs.

They hustle us all off to the cave and tie us up, leaving us for dead, I guess.

Gorman and his guys take my keys and my jeep and leave in a cloud of dust. He could have said, "So long, suckers," but he didn't.

In my mind, this was to be an easy in-and-out exercise, but no, we're the losers, Nathan, Jabari, Abdoullah, Dad, and I, tied up in a cave in the south-eastern mountains of Sinai. If you want to find us on a map, we're near Wadi Maghareh.

I feel doomed. No one will find us here anytime soon.

CHAPTER THREE
LOST IN SINAI

It's cooler in the cave than outside by about ten degrees, which is a lot when it's forty-five degrees in the shade and there isn't any. For several seconds, I think, *This is it. I will die in an ancient cave in Sinai.*

I look around. Small veins of turquoise are visible in the tunnel's walls. I visualize men working here thousands of years ago, trying to find that elusive piece of beautiful turquoise gemstone. Right now, I have little hope. Perhaps the workers had little hope too.

What can we possibly do next? I wonder. I don't have long to think because Nathan is hopping over. "Back-to-back now, with our hands together." I do as he says. "Any luck you can pull my rope?" he says and smirks.

"Well, you just may be in luck," I reply. I find the end and pull on the rope; I work on it, and it finally loosens.

With his hands free, Nathan undoes me, then we untie the others. I'm so glad to get my feet free.

"No sense looking for their vehicles, is there? Would they have left keys in them?" I ask.

"We could find a vehicle and hotwire it," Jabari suggests.

Nathan jumps in. "We don't know if they left a vehicle anywhere near."

"There's the scarab," I state.

"Are you crazy?" Nathan asks. "We want to get out of here."

"I have a plan," I state. I reach down in my pants. "Nothing here." The guys laugh. "But I might just have something here." I pull my foot out of my boot and the scarab hits the floor of the cave. Luckily, it doesn't break. "That feels better."

"Jonathan, it's a good thing you're clever," Nathan jabs.

"Dad, Nathan and I tested the scarab at home," I say. "We swirled into the past using your silver Horus and ended up in a tomb. There we met a guy who was having his tomb painted with an image of himself, and he was seated at a table loaded with bread and wine. Just to stress his importance, he had four ships painted under his chair."

"I know that tomb; I discovered it. Wahtye was the owner of the tomb, and it's where I found that silver Horus. The Egyptian government gave it to me in appreciation," Dad explains, always the historian.

"Wahtye's bodyguard wasn't terribly glad to see us," I state. "Now, I think we should be able to shoot back into the past and end up somewhere with people. I wonder if we put our hands on the scarab and I connect to the hieroglyphs on the cave entrance if the scarab will work. We could get help from the God of Life, Khepri-Ra, if we need him. I saw him carved on the walls."

"I thought that scarab had special power," Abdoullah confesses, smiling.

"So, we end up in the Middle Kingdom in Sinai. What then?" Dad wonders aloud.

"We know they mined heavily here for copper and turquoise. They must have had food, water, and transportation."

"Found your gun," Nathan shouts from off in the rocks. "I watched where the hired guy threw it."

"Okay, let's try. See if my plan works. Stand close together guys."

We stack our hands on the scarab and I place my right hand on the wall carvings of the god. I hope for the best. I'm relieved when the light in the cave shoots to black, then flashes with the same bright light as before. I can feel myself swirling round and round. Whoosh! What a rush!

I exhale as we land in a pile on the rocky ground. All around us are slaves working the mine. They stop work and look at us, awestruck. (Yeah, that's the right word, or maybe dumbfounded.)

"Oh my god, Jonathan, that scarab works," Dad says. He's surprised. I guess he was just going along with his crazy son.

Jabari comes over. He stares at the scarab. "That carved beetle is glowing. Mr. Jonathan, where did you get this magic thing?"

Before I can answer or the slaves react to our presence, my father yells in ancient Egyptian, "Who's in charge here?"

A muscular guy, I guess 1.68 metres tall, saunters over from a group of working men. I only know because I'm 1.83, six feet.

"What do you want?" the foreman challenges. The guy must be used to giving orders.

"What's next, Dad?" I ask.

"We need a way to get out of here," Dad says.

"I am thinking donkeys," Abdoullah says.

"Good idea." Dad turns to the foreman. "We want to buy some donkeys. Could you sell us five?" Dad asks.

"Do you have gold?" the foreman asks casually.

"Well?" Dad looks at me.

"Oh, sorry, the only word I understood was donkey. Hee-haa" I state.

"He wants gold," Dad says.

I turn back to Abdullah and Nathan. "Well, any ideas? Can you guys come up with anything?"

Abdoullah has a gold chain around his neck. He takes it off.

"I bet this is special," I realize. "Can you part with it?" I look at him closely and see from his face that someone special must have given it to him.

"I don't want to stay in Sinai," he grins. "We need to make it to another place."

I give the heavy gold chain to the guy in charge.

He, of course, wants more. I take off a gold ring my grandfather left me. Family heirloom. I just yank it off without a second thought because, as Abdoullah says, not giving it up might mean staying in Sinai. Well, what do you do when you're stuck?

"That's all we've got, Dad."

The man seems satisfied and hands over five donkeys. They come complete with blankets since there are no saddles on donkeys.

"Oh, what a sweet ass," laughs Nathan, patting his donkey.

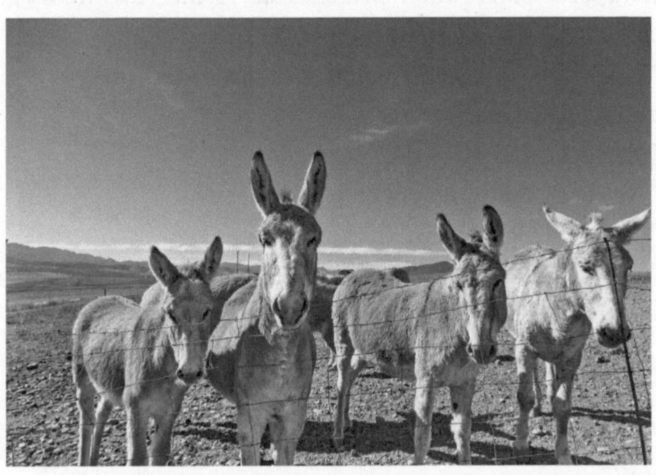

We barter for some food with shirts and things from our backpacks, then get on our donkeys.

I don't know if you have any experience riding donkeys, but they're different from horses. They're shorter, so they seem immediately bigger around. I mean, your legs can't go down and sort of just stick out. You can easily slide off because there are no stirrups like horses. Another thing: they have a mind of their own. You know how they say stubborn as a mule? Well, donkeys are cousins.

Okay, enough about donkeys. I know they aren't racing cars, but we're stuck back in time in a desert. We start heading north out of Sinai.

"Nathan, you're falling behind," I call back to him after a few minutes.

"He or she is stubborn. Doesn't want to go."

"That's what you are to do with your switch!" Abdoullah calls out helpfully.

One, two, three swats. "Still doesn't want to—" Nathan begins. Suddenly, his donkey breaks into a gallop. "I'm off!" he yells.

"Now he's passing everyone!" Jabari laughs.

So, we are off over the rugged sand, rock, and windswept Sinai. We ride for several days but are soon running out of water. We trudge on, and soon we see a Bedouin camp. These people are very helpful. The water they share with us isn't great, but it is water. They're wonderful people to give us water, a precious gift in a desert.

Finally, it seems we've made it. "I see it," Dad announces from the lead donkey, "it" being the Suez end of the Red Sea.

"All we have to do is find a temple or ruin," I say, "and we can be back in the present"

From the cliffs overlooking the Nile valley, the ancient city seems close, but we soon learn otherwise. We pick our way through the marshes at the end of the Red Sea and finally, many long, hot kilometres later, we ride into the city of Inebu-hedj, the White Walls, called Memphis by the Greeks.

I am so damn glad to escape that dusty plain. Just being near the city is great. As we ride in, we see the famous temple of Ptah, Hut-ka-Ptah (enclosure of the soul of the god Ptah.) In its day, it was reported to be the largest temple in the world, and it is huge. This ancient wonder is right before us. We get to see it now!

"How do you think we will ever get in there?" Nathan moans.

"Oh, suck it up!" I reply. "We're so covered in Sinai dust, no one will ever notice we're foreigners."

"Right you are," Dad says, supporting me. "No one can even see that we're not dressed like locals."

"We may not even have to get inside," I think aloud, looking at the paintings on the walls next to the gates.

Leaning against an outside wall decorated with gods and kings, we get together.

"Look," Dad exults, "artists have just painted these portraits of Djoser with his wife Hetephernebti and his mother, Nimaathap. And this is Ptah, who they are worshiping."

"Who was the king?" Jabari asks, pointing at the huge figure on either side of the gates.

"Ah, that is King Djoser, an interesting man. He built the famous step pyramid at Saqqara."

"Not now, Dad," I interject. "Save your lecture for university, I want to get back to the present."

"But I would like to learn more," Jabari states firmly.

"I would too, but I see a group of inquisitive worshippers, including some guards, gathering and looking at us." I encourage everyone to get on with the plan. "Let's get back to the present before we're arrested."

"Now, are you sure this will work?" Dad says with doubt in his voice.

"No, Dad, I'm not, but it always seems to. Have faith!"

I put my hand on the painting of the God Ptah. We clasp our hands on the scarab. The light outside fades quickly to black, then once again flashes brightly. I can feel myself swirling around and become dizzy. I try to keep my hand on the temple wall. Suddenly, it's not there! I almost fall over.

CHAPTER FOUR
COME ON, DAD, YOU'VE LOST YOUR MARBLES

We're back! In a ruin outside of Cairo, we see all that is left of Ramesses II Hall of Columns, built thousands of years later than the temple of Hut-ka-Ptah. Egypt's history is thousands of years long, and the Hall of Columns has now become a park.

"We're here!" Nathan booms out when he sees cars driving by beyond the park. He high fives everyone.

Somewhere in the past are five donkeys wandering around, is what I'm thinking about.

"I've taken tourists here many times," Abdoullah remembers. "They are always disappointed. A great city and temple gone, but the statues here and in the gardens are wondrous. It that how you say it?"

"Yep, 'wondrous,'" Nathan confirms.

"It is sad that the temple with its white walls and the later pillared hall no longer exist," Abdoullah states, looking around. "We must look at the famous Ramesses statue. There are two; one is here and the other one is moving around."

"You mean it has come to life?" Jabari asks, his eyes wide in disbelief.

"No, he was here, then they moved him to the circle in front of the train station and now he is in the entrance to the Grand Egyptian Museum."

That seems to satisfy Jabari.

Abdoullah guides us to the statue here in its own museum. "You will first see the statue has lost its lower legs, but even without them, it is incredible at ten metres in length. Because it is lying down, you can see the king's facial features closely up." We enter and stare down at the colossus. His face is incredible, the commanding features, the high fore head, his lips are perfect, his shoulders powerful, but the overall effect is pride. 'I am the powerful king of the Egyptian empire.' I can't wait to see its twin at the GEM.

"Now what?" I voice my thoughts, wanting to get going.

A city bus pulls up on the street across the gardens. Of course, it's loaded, but we run and get on anyway, just like the locals, and hang on. Then we jump off in the city centre, rent a jeep with a credit card stuffed deep in Nathan's pocket, and head back to keep our promise to Dr. Bernoune. Five men reporting for work.

Our trip back to camp is a brief ride across the plain of Saqqara. It ends with everyone relaxing over coffee in the mess tent at Saqqara, the new site for the next dig.

"I was surprised when you didn't call me a jerk for promising Dr. Bernoune that you and I would join his dig when we got back with Dad. I didn't have any right to promise you would stay and work here," I confess to Nathan.

"No worries! I'm fine with it. In fact, I'm really looking forward to working here for a season. But I've been wondering if we shouldn't also be thinking of our futures," Nathan says, looking very serious.

"Well, surprisingly, I've been thinking about that too. Since we're here, I think we should consider the American University in Cairo. I hear they have some great courses."

"Worth a look," Nathan agrees.

Dr. Czerny takes that moment to come into the mess tent. "Jonathan, Nathan, is that you under all that dust? I wanted to talk to you about our plans for this dig."

"We'll hit the showers soon. First, we need food! I don't recommend a donkey trek across Sinai."

"So you went to Sinai?" Dr. Czerny responds. "That's where you found your dad?" he asks.

"Yes, my father finds it easy to go missing."

Dad, having had a shower, comes over to the table where we're enjoying our supper.

"Jonathan, now that we're back, I'd like your help," Dad says in an unusual tone. I'm flattened; why is Dad asking for my help? Why is he suddenly talking to me like an adult?

"Let's hear it." I try to sound like this is an everyday thing. I beckon Nathan and Abdoullah and they join us.

"I lost it," Dad confides. I think he means his mind and now I wish I hadn't asked Abdoullah and Nathan to join us.

"I'm sorry, but after all you've been through, it's natural."

"No, it's not what you're thinking."

"Okay, lost what?" Why is Dad making it so complicated?

"I'm embarrassed. It seems I'm not . . . I'm not in control of . . . I'll just be straight. Gorman or some thugs of his came to our excavation of Tausret's temple. They stole the section of an obelisk and a cornerstone we had excavated. They're both inscribed with her cartouche, and therefore very valuable and important to our research. I hired a guard, but he wasn't of much use. The government states I am responsible, as I had possession of the blocks."

"And how can we help?"

"I realize that after saving me from Gorman in Sinai, you're more capable than I thought, and perhaps you could apply your skills and find the stolen blocks."

I look at Nathan and Abdoullah. They nod in agreement. Now we're detectives!

"We're on it," I say. "Abdoullah, get a hold of Hasaan and tell him to bring the van."

Jabari is hanging about. "Jabari, you're with us," I call out to him. "From the looks of you, you haven't had a shower either."

The four of us head for the showers, get dressed, and return to discuss the missing blocks with Dad.

"Is there anything else we need to know?" I ask Dad.

"Yes, quite a bit. Here are photos I took of the blocks. And they had to have a truck with a winch to steal those blocks," he adds. "I think we made a big mistake in having a press conference," he said. "Tausret was a minor pharaoh, but she was one of the few ruling female pharaohs and almost unknown to the public. Therefore, something from her temple makes a sensational story for the press. The thieves must have seen the information from the press conference and arranged the theft."

"Right, we're on it."

Hasaan shows up with the van and we pile in (as they say).

As we drive back to the south, Abdoullah fills us in. "So, you need to understand, there were many temples built here. The one preserved is called Medinet Habu. That's the Arabic name people call it by today. Its real name is 'Djeme.' Translated, that means mothers' and fathers' temple. This is where the ancients believed the very first four gods of Egypt were buried and, afterwards, were worshipped. So many kings, Ramesses III and others, one of them a woman, built their temples here." Abdoullah has reverted to his role as tour guide. I think he forgot he told us some of this before. He probably just starts his spiel automatically when he gets to a historic site.

"Who were the first four gods?" I ask Abdoullah. My favourite tour guide had a strange look on his face. "In the very beginning darkness covered the Primeval Ocean. Atum, whose spirit always existed decided it was time for creation to begin. An island emerged from the water, a mound for beginning and Atum called forth Ra, the sun god."

"Well, that doesn't tell us who the rest of the gods were," Jabari says.

"Yes, there is more to the beginnings." Abdoullah continues, "Ra had great power and he knew there needed to be much more so he created Shu the God of Air and Tefnut the Goddess of humidity. These two gods became parents to Geb, the Earth, and Nut, the sky. they are the four gods 'Djeme' the mothers and fathers."

Abdoullah looked at his audience and they were all asleep, accept of course me, so I could tell the story and our driver who was wide awake.

Finally we were at Luxor and stopped for tea and coffee. Now we zip across the bridge to Medinet Habu and the excavation of Tausert's temple.

With my directions—Dad told me where they excavated—we come to a tent. Inside we find a man on guard duty. I hope he isn't being paid because he's asleep. I shake him and, without thinking, start asking questions. I'm getting nowhere; he doesn't understand a word I'm saying. Then I show the man my father's picture on my phone.

The man's eyes light up as soon as he sees it and he relays a steady stream of Arabic. I call to Abdoullah.

"What's he saying?" I ask.

"He is saying he and my cousin worked together and helped at a dig with your father and several men who were working here."

"And then? What happened?"

"Some men came with a crane on a very sturdy truck and took two enormous stones."

"Does he know where they were taken?"

"He says the men came from the Luxor government. They told them that."

"This makes no sense. Ask him again."

We get the same answer.

We thank him. Abdoullah suggests giving the man baksheesh (a tip) so I dig in my pocket. Then we head back across the Nile to the government building.

Nathan, Abdoullah, Jabari, and I enter the air-conditioned building while Hasaan waits outside. It's very impressive with its marble floors and polished granite panels. I wonder if it were built when the British were influential here. The building has a very permanent feel.

I tell the receptionist our story, emphasizing we are looking for some important blocks taken from Tausret's temple at Medinet Habu. She says she'll have to telephone Cairo to inquire.

I lose it at that point. "But they were brought right here! In fact, your ministry made a public announcement when the Egyptologists discovered a block in the temple courtyard with the cartouche of Her Majesty Tausret. I need to see someone who can sort this mess out." I pause and smile. "Please!" I ask nicely.

The mood changes. The receptionist smiles. 'Please' did it. She says, "Have a seat. I'll see if the director will see you about this matter."

So, we sit in the director's waiting room. I look out the window and see the red car. Before I can tell the others, a young woman arrives from the inner office. My first impression is "wow." Her long, black hair is shining in the light streaming in through the window. Her dark eyes seem to sparkle. She has applied just the nicest shade of red lipstick to some very—well, you get the picture. She is just about twenty. So young for a government official. Yeah, you could say I'm stoked.

"I'm sorry to have kept you waiting. My name is Zahra Ishmahel. I am familiar with the situation since it happened in the Luxor district."

"I'm upset that you won't tell us what happened to the two blocks my father found! Look, you even notified the press about finding blocks with the pharaoh's cartouche on them."

I realize I'm shouting. I get the look. No need to shout. I take a deep breath and calm down.

She continues, "I will be glad to help you. We have a new government of which I am a representative, and we do not want to be embarrassed by this. These precious items you are looking for are missing, including part of an obelisk, and we would like to know where they are. Perhaps you can help us by retrieving them? Do you have an Egyptian Egyptologist on your team."

"Yes, Dr. Bernoune is an Egyptian. I can get a letter from him if that would help. He and my Dad, Dr. Darryl Johnsten, are working together on the excavation of Tausert's temple."

"Then Dr. Bernoune 's name will be on the excavation permit?"

"Yes, of course. We will hope to find them, clear my dad's name, and give you what belongs in the Luxor Museum."

"What's an obelisk?" Nathan asks as we leave the government offices.

"It's a tall, needle-like stone shaft with a pointed end, covered with hieroglyphs," I say.

"There's one in London. I've seen it," Nathan says.

"One point for you. Stolen from Kharnak or saved, depending on your point of view."

Abdoullah seems to know where to go next. Why? I'm not sure.

"You said the guard knew your cousin," I say. "Abdoullah, which cousin do we need to find?"

"Well, I have many cousins."

"Yes, I know that, but which one does the guard know?"

"Ah, Baahir, that is my cousin you want."

"Why not phone him?"

"Baahir?"

"Yes. Phone him."

"I am thinking like a taxi driver, just drive around to make the trip longer and charge more."

I look at Nathan, and we laugh. Well, we needed some humour.

Abdoullah phones. "No answer!" I think from Abdoullah's reaction, he knows something. He gets back on the phone.

We drive to Baahir's home, which Abdoullah locates through the Egyptian telegraph, and when we get there, we meet his wife, who says he will be back soon.

We get back in the van. Abdoullah says, "That was Egyptian talk. He won't be back soon. He is at the coffeehouse, the 'ahwa.' We call the water pipe, smoking shisha, our second wife. Men stay so long with her." He looks at me. I understand what he means.

"I know I'm uneducated, so what is 'shisha?'" Nathan asks, smirking.

"Tobacco mixed with molasses and fruit flavouring. Smoked through a water pipe," Abdoullah informs us.

"That's why you understood where Baahir is," I say with a grin.

We find Baahir at the ahwa, just as Abdoullah predicted. He's a short, hefty guy. He's in an excellent mood and is happy to see us. Of course, he would be happy to see anyone.

"As-salaam Alykum," he greets us.

Since he's being formal, Abdoullah responds, "Wa Alaykum as-salam. I am trying to help these two young men, who are strangers in our land, find the stones their father dug up at Medinet Habu. I am hoping you, with your expert knowledge of everything that goes on in Egypt, can tell us what happened to the stones they dug up."

The flattery works. Baahir answers, "Of course I know. The men from the government seized them."

I immediately get Abdoullah to ask again. "Please tell him that the government says they were stolen. No one from the government took the stones from the temple of Tausret."

After the translation back and forth, Baahir repeats, "The men said they were from the government."

"If only we had a clue where they were really from." Nathan mumbles.

Abdoullah picks up on that and asks Baahir if he noticed anything unusual.

Baahir says he was very suspicious of these "government men." He thought something wasn't right. He looked at the men and their vehicle carefully. He believes he has a clue.

"What is it?" Of course, he has to draw this out!

Abdoullah asks him and Baahir answers, "There was a sign on the truck, 'Rising Star of Misr.'"

"'Misr' is another name for Egypt." Abdoullah tells us.

"How do we find that company?" I ask.

Baahir loudly asks all the men in the awah.

Finally, an answer comes back from one man at the back, who is enjoying his shisha. "The Rising Star of Misr is in Zeitoun."

"Ah yes," smiled Abdoullah. "I know it well, a cou—"

"Of course," I say, "a cousin of yours works there."

"No, but just down the street from there. How did you know?"

Nathan and I enjoy the laugh and Abdoullah catches on. He laughs his deep belly laugh.

We get back in the van and off to Zeitoun.

As we drive along a narrow but busy road, Abdoullah notices Gorman's little red car following us. He tries to lose him but is unsuccessful. Abruptly, the car swerves in front of our van, forcing Abdoullah to brake and stop just inches from a street stall.

Abdoullah jumps out and shouts, "May the fleas of a thousand camels infest your armpits!" He's waving his fists in the air as the car disappears.

"I didn't believe people used that curse. I thought it was a joke," I say.

"It is no joke; it is a true. And I meant it!"

Once we're back on track, Nathan wonders aloud, "What are we going to do when we get there?"

Always organized, I say, "I think, Abdoullah, you need to tell the manager at the Rising Star of Misr that we're very rich Americans looking to buy some rare Egyptian artefacts to add to our collection. What do you think?"

"It is the good idea," Abdoullah says.

"Let's do this!" I say. I hope this will be an in-and-out job. Then I think of Sinai.

We find the Rising Star of Misr without any trouble. It has a gated yard with several sheds and booths around it. We locate the manager in a shed marked "Office," near the gate.

Once the manager hears Abdoullah mention the word "rich," he takes us over to a shed, where he says, "This is where I have my very best items."

After looking them over, I state, "Very nice, very nice, but we are hoping to buy an obelisk or even part of one and would pay the top asking price."

Abdoullah translates. The manager smiles at us and takes Nathan and me to a shed behind the one we were just in.

Nathan smirks. "The old shed behind the shed trick!"

As we walk to the shed, the sky grows darker and then lower. Then Set appears out of the clouds. He bares his teeth and gnashes them. He raises his WAS sceptre and points it towards us.

"Nathan, do you see him?" I yell.

"Yes, do you have any idea what we should do?"

Set starts laughing, "You have lost your protector, Jonathan," he says, his voice echoes against the surrounding buildings.

Piercingly loud clicking follows this as my champion, Khepri, with the power of Ra, swoops down in his purple cloud. His voice booms, "Take your deceitful tongue and vanish, Set, for I and my partner, the God Ra, will smite thee."

I can see he has his own WAS in one hand and an ANKH in the other.

Set fades reluctantly into the dark clouds as the bright sun, Ra, shines in the sky.

"Did I hear Set laughing?" Khepri asks, knowing he did.

"He said I had lost you as my protector," I respond.

"Deceitful, he is always deceitful. There are those in your world and mine who try to win by deceit, lies."

Khepri ascends to join his partner. Their combined light is brighter still.

"I never quite get used to that," Nathan states.

I nod my head. "No, I don't either."

We continue on to the farthest shed and find some large blocks, including one that could have been part of an obelisk. I get down on my hands and knees and begin reading the hieroglyphs and find the cartouche of Tausret.

"Here it is! Tausret." I shout excitedly.

That's when the lights go out. My big mouth. I didn't even see anyone come into the shed.

***

When I come to, I have no idea how long I was unconscious for. I see Nathan lying on the floor next to me. I put my hands on my throbbing head but realize it won't do much good to hold it. I sit still for several minutes, then get up and stand still until my vision clears. I realize we are in another shed without the blocks. I walk to the door and, of course, find it locked. Still feeling dizzy, I sit on the floor next to Nathan and hope my best friend will wake up. I read somewhere it's not a good idea to move someone who might have a concussion, so I just wait. And wait. I don't know what might happen next.

Eventually, Nathan moans. "What the hell happened?" he says as he holds his head.

"Two-by-four to the head," I answer, holding up the offending piece of lumber.

We try to open the door again, but someone has nailed it shut. I think these crooks figured out we are not who we said we are.

"We're muscular guys," I assert. Nathan and I put our shoulders to the door. It moves a bit. "If you use your brute strength and I use my shoulder, we can open this enough so I can jam this board into the opening. I think we can pry this sucker open."

We shove, we pry, and the door won't open. Then I hear Abdoullah yelling.

Finally, we give the door one last major push. The door opens and there, smiling at us, are Abdoullah and two police officers.

"You could have helped!" I say, challenging them. "And why were you yelling, Abdoullah?"

"The red car gang drove in here and parked against the door of the shed you were in. Fortunately, the police arrived. Miss Zahra sent them."

"She has a cell phone!"

"Yes, you are right."

"What else kept you?"

"We were loading the stones into the truck," Abdoullah explains with a grin.

"Thanks, Abdoullah. You did well organizing this. Let's go back to the dig and give the blocks to Dad for his research."

"I think we can say, 'Well done, guys!'" Nathan boasts.

"You're right again, bro."

***

When we arrive back at the dig in Hasaan's cab, with Abdoullah following behind in the truck with the two missing blocks, Dad comes running out.

"You are a wonder. How did you do this?"

"It's long and complicated. Ply us with drinks some evening after work and we'll fill you in."

He laughs There's no chance of that.

"Just so you know, the government has claimed them," I quickly add, still surprised that Dad praised me saying: 'you're a wonder.'

"Just as soon as I'm done with them, they'll go off to the Luxor Museum," Dad assures us.

Just then, Dr. Czerny shouts at us from across the parking lot. "There you are! Where have you been? You four left without permission and have held up this dig. Time is too precious for you to take off on some kind of joy ride. Consider yourselves suspended."

Nathan, Abdoullah, Jabari and I look at each other. "What?" we each say.

CHAPTER FIVE

PEPI ANKH'S TREASURE

After Dad explains to Dr. Czerny where we were and what we were doing, he shows him Tausret's blocks, which Dr. Czerny had never expected to see again. The older Egyptologist realizes we were not just off having fun. It was a significant learning experience. The most important thing learned: communicate! I should have let the boss know what we were doing. Why didn't Dad tell him?

Dr. Bernoune comes over and shakes our hands, "I think you have done us a great service. I was so glad when we dug these up that we had proof and then they disappeared." He goes back to the temple site whistling.

We take a well-deserved break, recovering from the crazy trip all around Cairo. We pay Hassan and promise to call him the next time we need an expert driver.

Nathan and I are just finishing breakfast the next morning when Dr. Czerny finds us. "Ah, here you are."

"Were we supposed to be somewhere?" I ask, feeling guilty without knowing why.

"I thought you might still be napping after your adventure," Dr. Czerny states. "We think you need to be thrown in at the deep end, as they say. You young men have impressed us. When we chatted earlier, you said you are thinking about the American University in Cairo. Jonathan, your father and I have arranged for you two to get field work credit for work being done with me.

"Now, as you are getting credit for this, I think you and Nathan should do the prep for this next dig. You will excavate the small pyramid in King Djedkare's pyramid complex. See what you can find out about it. You also need to go to Luxor and get signed onto the dig permit."

Now Nathan and I are off to the government offices in Luxor. We take Abdoullah with us in case we need someone to translate.

It surprises me again that the government offices in Luxor are so large, but it *is* the government building for the entire province. The receptionist smiles at me and says she will inform the director we are here.

"Thanks very much," I reply to her courtesy.

Soon, Zahra comes out of the inner office.

"We meet again," she says. I'm afraid I might act awkwardly meeting her again. *Get a grip, Johnsten,* I say to myself, *and try to relax.*

"I'm going to be doing fieldwork with the team at Abousir. This is Nathan Grant, my co-worker. Oh, I'm being a goof. You met before. These are Dr. Czerny's copies of the papers for the team." I hand them over. "He asked me to request our names be added to ensure we're doing everything legally." I believe I'm staring; I force myself to stop.

"Yes, I would be glad to add your names," Zahra replies. "First, I'll need to see your passports." We hand them over.

"You know, your English is excellent," I praise her. I can't take my eyes off her. Her smile is wonderful.

"I spent a year working at the Egyptian Embassy in Ottawa, as I needed to improve my English from the level I had at school here," she explains. "Now, signing here is just a formality because Dr. Czerny told us he might add more names to the file. It's nice to see that young people are getting involved."

I swear she's checking me out. Not obviously, but you know, her eyes meeting mine, her hand touching mine when she hands me the forms and again when she gives me back my passport. Of course, I can't stop grinning.

"I know this is a bit unusual, but, ah, would you consider going for coffee with me sometime?"

It sounds so lame. I'm embarrassed but try not to look it.

"Yes, it might be unusual, but I have a brief break right now. You can share my tea outside on the bench in the square."

I look at Nathan and Abdoullah. Abdoullah says right on cue, "Nathan, I have a cousin here. I want you to meet." Such smart guys.

Zahra and I walk over to the neighbouring square, a little park really. We sit on a bench surrounded by palms and jasmine and other flowering shrubs. We chat about the usual stuff: the weather here, the weather in Ottawa, crazy cold winters.

"You should try Vancouver. Much better weather," I say.

"I always meant to get out to see the Pacific coast but couldn't fit in a trip." She seems genuinely sorry.

After a few minutes, I realize she probably has to get back to work soon, but I can't leave not knowing if I'll ever see her again. "I don't know if you're interested," I say, "but we're investigating a tomb this week. Hasn't been worked on for about forty years. You're welcome to come if you can get a day off."

"I've never been invited before," she replies quickly. "I studied hieroglyphs at university. The language always fascinated me, so I'm very interested."

"Like interested how?" I paused. "That's not very good English, but you know what I mean."

She smiles. I smile. So silly.

"I am interested in knowing more about any dig in Saqqara."

"Okay, well, I'll text you before we open the tomb then," I reply.

Out of nowhere, the red car that was chasing us at the airport in Luxor pulls up. Three guys jump out and one of them is Gorman. He starts running towards me from the far side of the park. Then I notice one guy has a gun. This supposed to be a quiet chat in the park. What the hell is going on?

"Get down!" I yell and help Zahra get under the bench just before Gorman grabs me.

"Okay, Johnsten," Gorman says, "give me the scarab." I look around expecting Set to appear.

"Oh, like I carry it with me." I'm unafraid even though he's pointing a hand gun at me. I'm filled with the purpose of keeping Zahra safe and standing up to Gorman. I've had enough of this guy. I think I've said that before.

At that moment, two guys with automatic rifles rush into the park. They yell in Arabic before firing a few shots. There is blood everywhere as they kill Gorman's henchmen right in front of us. Gorman somehow dodges the bullets and takes off, the weasel.

I help Zahra up from under the bench. I stand there enjoying holding her hand.

"Wow, I wasn't expecting that. You know, I sensed we were being watched. Where did those guards come from?" I ask.

"All elected representatives have bodyguards who try to be here but not here, if you know what I mean. In this case, you brought trouble, and they dealt with it."

"Nice to have that kind of protection."

Abdoullah and Nathan come hurrying up the street to the park. I realize I'm still holding Zahra's hand and let go.

"Just having a nice, quiet chat, are you? Does anyone know these bodies?" Nathan asks.

The event leaves us shocked. Then we realize there is humour in Nathan's question.

When we stop laughing, I say to Zahra seriously, "If you come to our dig, I think it will be quieter than this."

"I would hope so!" she says. We laugh.

"We'd really be honoured to have a government official visit our dig," I say.

The police collect the two bodies, we walk to another corner of the park, and then Zahra goes back to work. Nathan, Abdoullah, and I go back to camp where I text Zahra, "Tomorrow should work for a visit. Sorry for the short notice, but the team is ready to go."

She texts back, "Tomorrow works really well. Send a map so I can find you."

I have a hard time getting to sleep. I get to see Zahra again tomorrow. She's so beautiful, so sophisticated. I text a map of the area then finally doze off.

***

I go for breakfast at the mess tent and meet up with the guys. We really chow down, excited by opening a new tomb.

I start with, "Good morning, Nathan Grant and I are charged with giving you notes on this pyramid. This complex of pyramids belongs to King Djedkare and was therefore the tomb of a family member, like one of his wives or children or a noble he was honouring. Stay tuned for more."

We start early, focusing on the need to find the entrance to the tomb. There's a very narrow passage between two blocks that we realize must be the entrance, but it's not big enough to fit all our equipment through, so we get to work widening it. We work our way through many metres of rubble, using winches to move the blocks in front of the entrance, until we find the stone-framed entrance and stone floor leading to a corridor.

Dr. Czerny beckons me over. "Dr. Johnsten wanted to get started early this morning. We should find him when we get into the tomb."

What's that about? I wonder. Dad usually tells me what he's doing. And why would he go in through such a narrow passage on his own? He must know how dangerous that is.

Zahra arrives with her bodyguard and I introduce her to the Egyptologists. They are welcoming.

"Let's get in and see what this tomb is hiding," Dr. Bernoune says with encouragement. He gives Zahra, Nathan, Abdoullah, and me helmets with lights. "I cannot guarantee your safety," he tells us. He has a poker face, so I'm not sure if he's joking or not.

The tomb has a long flight of stairs carved into the rock and a pleasant sort of basement smell. I don't know how else to describe it. The walls in the entrance are encased in very fine limestone polished to perfection.

The deeper we go, the harder it is to breathe. Then, after the corridor, we come to a halt. There is a wall of blocks. Did Dad come in here? How could he have gotten through the wall? He couldn't have. What's up?

"This isn't very exciting, Zahra. Sorry," I apologize.

"This is still very interesting. What will you do next?"

"We'll hope there's a crack or small opening that might help with removal of some of the blocks that form this wall. Let's see if we can feel any air coming through anywhere," I say.

Nathan gets down on his knees, testing for any air flow. "Here, I can feel some air here. There's an opening."

"How big an opening?" Dr. Bernoune asks.

"Not huge, about four centimetres. Almost looks like a keyhole. Might fit a crowbar," Nathan relays.

I suddenly have an idea. "The ANKH is called a key, right? That's what we want here. I wonder . . ." I say as I fish around in my backpack. I find the ANKH the judge gave me in Vancouver. I shove the end into the small opening. Nothing happens.

"Let me try a way," Abdoullah whispers. He takes the ANKH from me and puts it in backwards, round end in first. Of course, it doesn't even fit.

"Well, that didn't work," I say. But the block slowly starts sliding towards us.

"What do you know?" Nathan cheers.

I swear Abdoullah has some connection to the gods. Magic! A block, hundreds of pounds in weight, slides out, albeit extremely slowly. I look at Zahra. She's marvelling at the magic and at the movement of the first block. She catches me looking at her and smiles.

"Help here," Nathan yells back out the corridor. Shortly, a couple of hefty guys come into the tomb bringing tools, their muscles, and some grease. Together, we slide the block out farther down the passage. Then the next block, and the next, until we have a large enough entrance. We use our helmet lights.

The passage behind the wall we're removing leads inside about three metres, or ten feet, into a decorated entrance. On either side of it, paintings of two men dressed in pleated skirts, holding staffs, guard it. Just beyond the entrance, there is so much gold on the furniture, boxes, and other objects in front of us that I'm shook. I look at the others. They have different expressions: some look on in awe while others seem stunned or excited. There are golden chests with beautifully decorated panels just inside the chamber.

On the walls on either side of the entrance to the next room are detailed paintings of guardians and columns of hieroglyphs. "Zahra," I ask, "Can you put your skills to work?"

"Oh, you remembered." She gives me a quick smile and starts working, "'The most noble Pepiank, Vizier of Middle Egypt, given many honours by the king, is owner of this tomb. Cursed be he who disturbs His life in the Field of Reeds,'" she reads. "Then it gives some of his titles: 'Honoured as Count by His Majesty, Chief Justice, Scribe of His Majesty, Sealer of the King, and Overseer of the Granary of Middle Egypt.'"

It takes us several minutes to recover from the importance of this man and his tomb, as well as from hearing the threat of the curse.

We then go into the main room of the tomb where there are beautiful gilt tables, chairs, and two beds with lions on each of the four legs stacked on top of each other. In the walls of the tomb are four serdabs, or alcoves, each with a statue of a god: a gilded statue of Thoth, God of Knowledge; one of Heka, God of Medicine and Magic, with two raised arms and wrapped by two golden snakes, the symbol of Ka; one of Osiris, the bright green God of Rebirth; and finally, Isis, the silver Goddess of Love. On the far wall is a false door. The "Ka," or soul of the tomb's owner, could pass through that door from his burial chamber. His statue is in the space framed by wonderful hieroglyphs, richly painted.

We set to work, with people from the Luxor Museum and our entire team, cataloguing on laptops everything we find in the tomb, itemizing and describing each item quickly, more quickly than previous excavation teams would have been able to. As the team removes the objects, we do the customary careful brushing. Then we sieve and brush the floor to collect beads or other small items, usually from parts of jewellery, that may have been dropped during a robbery. This tomb was so well sealed, we know a major robbery had not taken place, and we find nothing.

Then, around a corner, we break the seal on a door and discover another room. In its centre is a granite sarcophagus. Inside it, once we take off the lid, is a cartonnage coffin. The handsome face covered in gold leaf of the man, Pepiank, taking part of his king's name, Pepi, smiles as if created recently. There are stacked ivory-inlaid boxes full of jewellery around it, two and three boxes high, almost hiding the sarcophagus. They had not spent money on gold screens as in Tutankhamen's tomb.

"It is obvious that a man with all the titles I read would have acquired a lot of wealth to put in his tomb. No wonder he has such a treasure trove," Zahra says in admiration. "You suggested, when we started, this would not be very interesting, but the owner of this tomb put all his wealth in here. I can't understand how all of this can be the wealth of a normal man and not a king," Zahra states.

Then she and Nathan stare at me. "Okay," Nathan says, "What's wrong?"

"I've been so occupied with the discovery of this tomb that I've forgotten about Dad. He's gone missing again. This is crazy. I know he came into the tomb. He told Dr. Czerny he was coming here. I have no idea what to do.

"Take a deep breath. Together, we can find him again." Zahra says. I look at her. She is such a caring person. I am so lucky to find her.

The team works together and takes all Pepiank's wealth to the examination tent for cleaning and checking against the computer records made in the tomb. It will take the experts from the museum a long time to catalogue it and properly clean and restore it.

"So," says Nathan, "your dad still hasn't surfaced?"

I shake my head. Why hasn't he come to see this? I'm starting to worry. I look around the camp, in his tent, the washhouse, and the administration tent where his desk is.

Nathan finds me. "Come down to the cataloguing tent. We're celebrating."

I go, not having solved my problem. *Dad is missing again* I repeat to myself. Maybe if I give my head a shake. Not helpful.

After I thank Zahra for coming and get a kiss on the cheek, Nathan and I inspect some of the artefacts that need extra care with cleaning or repairing. There is so much gold and so many precious and semiprecious stones.

Dr. Czerny comes into the tent. "You can be very proud of your work and the results," He says, beaming.

This is as good as it gets, I think.

But I shouldn't have thought that! Suddenly, we hear shots out in the compound. Four men wearing scarves over their faces burst in with automatic assault rifles. They yell at us in Arabic and wave at us to get down on the floor. We lie down quickly, watching helplessly as they scoop up all the jewellery, solid gold, and alabaster or obsidian statues from the tables. They leave as fast as they came. Nathan and I quickly go out into the compound and find the security guards lying dead. I feel sick knowing these two guys gave their lives for our safety. I don't remember ever even acknowledging their presence. Not even a 'good Morning.'

The police arrive in about half an hour. Not bad for a trip across the river. All the artefacts stolen have been catalogued, so we can give them lists, even photos.

"Why don't we have camera security after all this time? The Egyptian telegraph knows what's happening, I'm sure," I complain to Dr. Bernoune. He looks loaded down with the responsibility and the awareness that I'm right. "Can I help?" I ask.

"Thanks, but the Department of Antiquities stated they would install it immediately. I should have checked to make sure they were doing it."

Weeks of work gone in a few minutes. Luckily, they didn't take the furniture or the beautiful chests.

Later, working on the floor of the passage, Jabari, being a very meticulous young man, finds a medallion. He brings it to me, and I immediately recognize it.

CHAPTER SIX
DAD? NOT AGAIN

"I know this medallion. It's my dad's," I say to Jabari. "He always wears it around his neck. We already know he couldn't get into the burial chamber, but this proves he was in the opening passage. Thanks so much Jabari. I am grateful for your help again!"

"Come on, guys. Let's get some air and food while I think." I beckon to Jabari, Abdoullah, and Nathan.

After checking the food table and grabbing a cup of coffee, I say to the guys, "All right. Where could Dad have gone and how? If he was in this tomb and then disappeared, it must have been magic. It was magic."

"Agreed," Abdoullah nods.

"Well, if I didn't know better, I'd say he had the scarab," I say. "We know it can do weird things, especially in a tomb. But it's here in my backpack," I state. All the time I'm thinking, *I always keep the scarab in my jeans.*

Nathan and Abdoullah look at me. *Are you sure?* their looks tell me.

"Okay. I'll check."

"Dump it out," Nathan urges as I begin rummaging through. I do as he says and dump everything out.

"Of course. No scarab!" Abdoullah exclaims, watching.

"Why would he go alone? I can't figure it out!" I say. I end up with my head in my backpack. "I can't be wrong!"

"Not the time to be funny, Jono. So, he's lost in the past," Nathan concludes. "With your scarab!"

"We need to find him!" I say. Now I'm panicking.

"Again?" Abdoullah looks incredulous.

"You're forgetting one little thing: we have no scarab." Nathan says, rubbing it in.

"I think," Abdoullah suggests, "we can use the ANKH. You said the judge called it a kind of a key."

"And it moved the blocks in the tomb," Nathan adds.

"Let's try that." I'm all ready to go. "What was Dad thinking? Going back in the past alone, not even telling us what he had planned. Worse than a teenager."

We had seen the excavation process at other digs and are aware it could take the crew weeks to finish cataloguing, cleaning, and transporting all the artefacts from the tomb to the museum. We ask Dr. Czerny for a few days off, and after thinking about it, he allows it.

We all heard Zahra read the hieroglyphs about the tomb's owner, Pepiank, a vizier during the long reign of Pepi I, which lasted forty years or so. The central government at this time was supposed to be stable, so we feel fairly safe going back in time again.

We go down to where the blocks were taken from. "How should we make this work?" I ask Abdoullah as I hold the ANKH.

"I rub it on my jellabiya," Abdoullah volunteers, gesturing to the loose-fitting article of clothing he wears.

"Okay, let's go for it," I say, ready for the challenge.

I give Abdoullah the ANKH and he rubs it. We each put a hand on it. It starts off working slowly, but the dark tomb soon brightens, then grows dark again. I can feel the familiar swirling motion. I begin to think this will work. We see an extra brilliant flash. Whoosh!

"We made it!" I exclaim. We're standing in Pepiank's tomb, but it's new. It's being painted and some furniture is being carried in.

Standing in front of us is a very important man.

"Im Hotep, Pepiank?" I ask as we bow. He isn't—or wasn't—a king, but he is important, as we had seen. What I had learned in preparation for this is that Pepi the First had ruled for a relatively long time. His grandson made history for reigning for ninety-four years. Of course, he became king at the age of six. During this period, courtiers had become powerful. Pepiank had taken on so many departments and so much responsibility that his titles took up a quarter of a page in a reference I consulted, but you've heard at least a third of them, and who knows what they all mean.

Pepiank beckons us and quickly leads us out of his tomb. We are in the way of his servants.

Looking stern, Pepiank asks in ancient Egyptian, "Why are you in my tomb? I should have you arrested for violation of a sacred space." He has led us into a large tent erected outside of his tomb. The tent is furnished with beautiful furniture. There are servants standing by, waiting for their master's commands. I think this tent has been erected for Pepiank's comfort any time he comes to visit his tomb.

"I take by your dress you are from a foreign land," he continues.

The studying I've been doing of Egyptian hieroglyphs during my evenings off must be paying off because I understand most of what he says.

I try to respond in my best Egyptian, "I am looking for a foreigner like me, older, my father. He came this way."

Pepiank calls out to someone. A handsome young man answers. Pepiank asks him if he is aware of a foreigner new to this area.

Well, it would be too easy if he had. The man leaves to find an answer. Before long, a guard appears. He looks at us suspiciously. We try to appear nonchalant.

"We found a strange foreigner in the cemetery of Inbu-Hedj. We put him to work in the field of Amun-Ra."

"Can I see him? He might be my father."

There is a bit of back and forth between the guard and Pepiank. Finally, Pepiank instructs the guard to take me to this man.

I give Nathan and Jabari a quick rundown on what the chat was about, although they could have guessed. Abdoullah helps me out. Then we go with the guard out of the capital by chariots.

The fields are green acres, irrigated from the Nile, planted with grain and cotton. Hundreds of men with captives among them are working here. We get to the temple and the fields that are attached to it. There, tied to a post, being whipped, is my dad. He is dazed, not even looking at me. I am near tears. My dad being whipped. I can't even imagine it.

"How can I buy this man's freedom?" I ask the overseer.

He scoffs at the idea. "There is no way that we can release this man. He has violated the cemetery by wandering among the mortuary temples of the kings."

"It is terrible he had no respect for the temples, the priests, or the gods," I state. "But this is an ignorant foreigner. I agree to take this foreigner away. What is his ransom?"

"He is old and unfit. We would want ten days of work from a healthy man like yourself."

"I can supply myself and three strong men to work for you for three days each."

The overseer mulls this over. "Four days. No more discussion."

"When do we start?"

"Tomorrow, just after dawn."

The next morning, just as the sun rises, Abdoullah, Nathan, Jabari, and I show up at the field where we saw Dad. The overseer gives us each a hand plow and puts us to work. We work all day in the scorching sun. Other slaves bring water, then bread and beer for lunch. Dad works alongside us and can work harder now that he has hope and is in our company. Some workers are working in return for help on their own land. The four days seem to crawl by. If we slow our work, whips urge us to work faster.

As we're leaving at the end of the fourth day with Dad, the overseer approaches me. "I need one more day's work for this man. I didn't know he could work so hard."

"We need to take this to a judge," I protest.

Pepiank's name helps us get a judge. I don't know if he has undue influence, but the judge hears the agreement we had with the overseer and then says, "The agreement has been fulfilled." He asks us to make an offering at the temple of Ptah. When I tell you "asks," I'm sure this is a request I can't refuse.

Before we leave, I confront my father. "I can't believe you would just leave without a word," I say.

"Okay, Jonathan, you know me. Is this my usual behaviour? Try Gorman coming to my tent in the middle of the night with one of his goons, and going to your tent, standing over your sleeping body with a gun, and taking the scarab. I resisted, but he threatened to shoot you. They knocked me around when the scarab wouldn't work. After being smacked around, I suggested going into the tomb."

"So where is Gorman now?" I ask.

"No idea. They left me in the cemetery here."

"I'll get you free before dealing with him. Need to make that offering first."

I go to the temple by chariot, driven by Nathan, leaving Dad with Abdoullah. The guards watch me to ensure I make the offering.

At the temple, I pick up on what to do by observing worshippers giving various gifts to Amun-Ra.

After leaving my "gift"—a couple of coins from our pockets that I put in the container—a very well-dressed young woman wearing a gold headpiece enters with an offering for the temple. This lady is very attractive. My mistake is I stay and "look her over," as they say. She gives a gift and seems to pray silently, but then, as she's leaving, she grabs my arm. I am Princess Ankenesmerire. You are a very fascinating young man. I want you." She waves at some strong looking men accompanying her and they hustle me outside and shove me towards a horse-drawn wagon.

Now, I guess I should be flattered. She checked me out, but I feel like a fish out of water: unsure of the language, the customs, and not sure what she might require a love slave to do. I'm sure I can guess though. As we approach the wagon, I yell, "I'm being kidnapped!" Nathan, Abdoullah, Dad and Jabari turn to look at me. I see Nathan turn the chariot around. The chariot was made for two but four of them are holding on afraid they would be flung off at any second. Their crazy movements were like kernels in a popcorn maker. They are following the wagon carrying the princess, her companions, and me.

The home of the princess is beautiful. Not that you'll ever have a chance to visit, but you can check out the great tomb paintings of the gardens. The house is set in a large garden surrounded by a wall. A T-shaped pond in front of the house includes bright coloured exotic species of fish. Fruit trees have been planted in front of the house and have their branches covered in blossoms supported on the trellises in front of the porch.

When we arrive and the guys step out of the chariot, we are greeted by her brother Prince Ankhaf who ensures we are all given a large goblet of beer. The home of the brother and sister of the royal family is beautiful and l and my friends stun Princess Ankenesmerire. Dad needs to sit down. He bows and finds a seat. I introduce Nathan, Abdoullah, and Jabari, and she seems to treat it as four-for-one day or something, checking us out with her eyes and hands. There is much giggling from her and flexing on our part. So much vanity. Drinks and food arrive as well as some female friends. Our lucky day. The prince has duties to perform and leaves the fun to his sister.

I'm guided to sit next to Ankenesmerire and cuddle up. While I drink beer, I wonder what we should do next. The princess strokes my leg, working her way up and working me up. I can't help it. I think my body is telling me what I should do next. She is so beautiful, and her kisses are fantastic. She beckons Nathan to come sit on her other side. He seems eager to please Her Highness. Abdoullah and Jabari have not been left out. Two curvaceous young women have found them attractive.

"Dad, do you have the scarab? We might need it to get back to the present." The Egyptians are a bit confused at not being able to understand me.

"A few more minutes won't hurt," Nathan protests. He kisses the princess again.

"Our mission is only half complete," I tell him.

"What do you mean, half?"

"Dad didn't come alone. He was brought!"

"Let me guess," Nathan says. "Gorman, and he has the scarab!"

"Right. You are a bright lad!"

"I've had time to think about how this all happened. And we have no idea where Gorman is now?"

"We need to get it back!" I say, and then pry Ankenesmerire's hand off my—me.

"Do you think the princess might help? I think she might like us to stay," I guess.

"Use your blue-eyed charm, Jono," Nathan replies.

So, we tell her she's beautiful, we love her, and then ask for her help. She thinks it would be a lot of fun to find this evil foreigner.

"Where would a robber find gold and jewels to steal?" I ask her. "That might be where the bad guy is."

Her answer, the result of tickling, kissing, and promises, is the Temple of Ptah in the centre of the city of Inebu-Hedj.

Leaving Nathan and Jabari to entertain the princess, and Dad to enjoy the party, Abdoullah and I take the chariot and drive into the city. We arrive to hear a great ruckus going on. We're in luck. Priests are yelling at Gorman and his goon, who are trying to grab golden statues from the temple. Have they no respect?

Abdoullah and I jump out of the chariot and take the whips from the chariot, lashing out at Gorman and the goon. We attack them both with the heavy handles. Who says you can't do things backwards. I knock Gorman with a handle. I'd like to do more to him, but he falls to the ground and I search him and grab the scarab from his jacket pocket. It was glowing a bit as if it recognized me. Weird. Now we're ready to quickly take off to rescue Nathan.

We arrive back to find Nathan nearly naked and the princess enjoying working her hands down from his chest. I pull him away.

"Sorry to interrupt," I tell the princess, "but we're here on a mission." We grab a beer from the princess' table and then we sit, drink beer, and chat, occasionally interrupted by the princess affectionate fingers.

"Did you get it?" Nathan asks, finding it hard to change focus.

"Yes. Where's Dad?" I ask. Nathan points. My father is being pushed onto a couch by a large woman who knows what she wants. "How are you doing, Dad?" I call to him.

"I really need help getting out from under," he begs. We distract the lady by stroking her cheek and kissing her ears. Dad crawls out from under.

We're all ready to leave when I have another idea. "Nathan, I wonder if you and some of the party guests would mind if the princess and I went away for a bit?" Is this a dumb question?

"How far is it to the palace of King Pepi?" I ask the princess.

She looks me in the eye. I'm sure she thinks I'm crazy. "Why do you want to know?"

"I would like to meet him. We didn't travel all this way for nothing." After I say this, I hope she doesn't consider herself nothing. But her reaction is startling. She starts laughing and can't stop.

She points at me. "You want to see the king?" she chokes. She needs to grab her drink.

"Common people cannot look at the king," the princess' friend, who is running her hand down my back, explains.

"Have you met him?" I ask the princess.

"Of course. Don't be so stupid. My father is the son of his body."

That shut me up. Then, on second thought, I decide to press on. "You know, Your Highness," I say, "since we come from the future, the king may want to talk to us."

The princess pats her perfect wig, rearranges her sheer dress, sits back, and thinks. "I don't want him to be mad at me and say, 'You silly girl, why didn't you tell me?' I'll just change so we can go for an audience at the palace."

Several minutes later, the princess reappears looking dazzling in an even sheerer dress, if that's possible, a gold enameled belt, and an extravagant wig topped with a tiara of golden cobras. "All right," she says, "come with me, handsome."

We get in a wagon and the princess and I are driven to the palace. The princess leans into me with a pay-attention look. "It is good to know kingship thrives on ceremony. They will check us when we arrive to make sure we are clean. Our feet will be washed. Maybe more of you," she says, giving me a sceptical look.

The palace is awesome, like super awesome. "What is this room where we are being lined up?" I ask.

"This is the Hall of Silence. It is the central court of the palace with thirty-two columns, decorated with the expeditions of the king. The paintings show Pepi I striding with mace in hand and enemies at his feet or the king riding in his chariot with bow at the ready and men with short black hair lashed beneath the axel.

People approach the king in two rows. We will go up to the throne room using the left aisle since I am of the royal family. The centre aisle is for the king alone. The far aisle is for others. Next we go into the vestibule where a priest wafts incense over us," Ankenesmerire tells me.

"Then can we meet him?" I ask but am told to hush as we start walking.

We head down the hall of silence and I'm like a kid at a carnival. There is a second hall of columns where the pillars are decorated with blue faience or fabricated glass running up the pillars in wide shining panels. All the walls are painted with scenes of gardens, including the floor. The dazzling throne room has shiny red columns topped by white papyrus leaf capitals detailed in gold.

The king, dressed in a stiff white kilt, has an elaborate gold sash wrapped around his waist. On his head is a helmet-shaped wig surmounted by what is called a "sheshed diadem." This stiff, decorated gold band has a cobra and vulture on the front and five ribbons that drape down the king's back. On his naked chest is a pectoral pendant of gold and lapis lazuli depicting the vulture goddess Nekhabet, the protector of Egypt. Seated in a gold-encased throne, holding his crook and flail, his feet in gold sandals, he looks resplendent. (Word nerd again.)

I'm feeling wobbly. Well, insignificant. I don't know if I can speak; I'm so wowed by the spectacle and splendour.

Princess Ankenesmerire bows very low, and I follow. We remain bent over for several seconds.

"Your majesty, I know this is unusual, but I have brought a stranger from the future to you so that I can inform you of his presence in your kingdom. He is open to any questions you might have."

"Thank you, Princess. Welcome, stranger. It has been some time since I have seen you, Ankenesmerire. I would like to see you this evening. Now, stranger, you are from the future?"

"Yes, your majesty."

"How did you come to be in Egypt now?"

"I have a Sacred Scarab. The God Khepri is my protector." I decide not to get into the whole crazy story. I can tell he's mulling this over. I guess he's interested or at least willing to give it a go.

"So, tell me of the future; what will happen during my reign?"

I'm trying to remember the reign of Pepi I. I think I'll tell him what I read on Wikipedia but leave out the bad parts.

"Your majesty will be remembered as a great builder. Your complex of pyramids for yourself and six of your wives, the building project known as 'Pepi Mennefer,' is famous. You will be known for your expeditions to the south and to the north to get resources. Accounts of these expeditions is found in writings four thousand years in the future. Beware of those who wish to gain power. There is a royal wife who is a threat!"

Well, talk about right on cue. I am rocked! A general and several guards rush in. I predicted a plot that has just been exposed! Weird.

"Speak, General Weni."

"My king, I heard gossip in the palace. An informant told me of the plot of the royal wife Sebwetet. She plans to kill your majesty and put her son in your place. I have brought this woman to you now." A guard brings in a very beautiful woman wearing a stunning diadem and massive gold necklace. She holds her head high, hiding any possibility of conspiracy.

"You, Sebwetet, the royal wife, great of affection, have plotted to kill me?"

The silence is pervasive. It's better than any movie I have seen. The palace, the costumes, the characters: a king, a queen, and a general and the dramatic tension. Wow!

Sebwetet stares at the king. She says nothing.

His Majesty instructs his general, "Have her taken to the place of justice. Summon a judge to try the accused." Looking directly at her, he says, "I think, Sebwetet, you may not see the setting of Ra."

I read that the king follows the written law, which is why he doesn't have her killed immediately. He, too, must await the results of a trial. The princess and I stand silently. His Majesty stares at me. I'm trying to think of something profound to say.

"You, foreigner, have predicted too well. The actions of my wife sadden my heart. What more can you tell me of the future?"

"History tells us that your trust in Khui, the Prince of Abydos, shows good judgement. Your trade with the Levant and mining for turquoise and copper in Sinai are profitable. Your program of temple building is memorable." I bow and move backward in respect. We leave his presence.

"Well, handsome," Ankenesmerire says, "that went well, and I have been summoned to the palace this evening. That may be profitable." The princess' wagon takes us back to her home.

"Do I have a story to tell you, Nathan!" I say.

"First, I really need to find a toilet!" Nathan states so emphatically I decide now is not a good time to chat. I'm not quite sure how to ask, but I get across the idea that we need to use a toilet.

The princess laughs again, but I'm not sure if it's because of my weak ancient Egyptian. I might have said, "we need to water the flowers," but we all leave at once, disappear around the outside of the house, and make for the chariots to take us to the temple where I hope the scarab will work. It likes a holy place, a tomb, whatever. I could have had more of being a love-slave for the princess though. Maybe next trip.

We ride to the temple where I finally hold my scarab and give it a good rub. We're so close to solving all our problems when the princess and her bodyguards surround us. I quickly put the scarab in my pocket where it throbs. I'll never leave it out of sight again! I'm trying to think of my options here, but the princess' guards—four big guys—look like they would love for us to start a fight.

"Come on back to the party," Ankenesmerire invites. Who am I to argue? We go to party. A servant pours me a goblet of wine. Quite nice too. The princess and her friends, men and women, pair up with us. The princess starts by feeding me fruit, then slowly removes my clothing, then hers and her guard's. She and I drink some more wine as music plays and the fountain in the pool comes alive and sprays a cascade high in the air. Her experienced hand causes nature to take over. It surprises me that the guard wants to be involved too. He's a cute young guy. I look around and find that Dad, Abdoullah, Jabari, and Nathan are all getting similar treatment.

I stand up: "Hey, what are you thinking! Are you just having a great time and forgetting we have people who are probably worried about us? And Dad, and that woman? No!"

The three guys join me. I collect Dad. I rub the scarab, which had been primed at the temple. The princess' guards try to control us.

I curse them. I'm not sure it will work, but I have read about curses. Holding the scarab in one hand and the ANKH, which one of my friends hands me, in the other, I yell out, "redi nihti khefti." The guards flee.

We finally put our hands on the scarab. The light does its thing—dark, then dazzlingly bright—and we experience the circles of time swirling, swirling, whoosh. We're dumped on the floor of Pepi Ankh's tomb in the present!

"What was the curse you put on those guys?" Abdoullah asks.

"Basically, 'death.'"

CHAPTER SEVEN

THE GREAT ROYAL WIFE

We walk the short distance back to the camp naked. It must be amusing or shocking to see us walking along, looking like paintings of Osiris with his penis exposed. We go into our tents to find clothing and then regroup in the mess tent.

"Dr. Czerny, I presume!" I smirk. "It's good to see you."

"I heard Dr. Johnsten was missing, so I came to help, but nobody was really sure what had happened."

"Well, Doctor, I'm right here," Dad jokes.

"Sit down, and we can chat over coffee," I suggest.

Dr. Bernoune joins us. "Darryl, you're looking thinner," he observes.

"Yes, a trip to the past can do that." Dad turns to me. "How did you get into the pyramid?" he asks.

I quickly respond, "A wise Egyptian scribe gave me an ANKH in Canada. Abdoullah figured out how to use it. It was literally the 'key' to unlocking the sealed wall. A few days later, after we helped with cataloguing the burial chamber, Jabari found your medallion on the floor in the passage leading down to the chamber. You disappeared and

I had proof." I flutter my fingers and make a "wooo" sound. "Magic. I guessed and hoped you left your medallion as a clue. We used the ANKH and went into the past to find you. I'm so glad it worked."

"Do you really expect me to believe this?" Dr. Bernoune says, smiling in disbelief. "That doesn't explain how your father went into the past."

"Well, Dr. Gorman stole my scarab. He took Dad with him. You see, I found a Sacred Scarab here in Egypt years ago and it has power."

"Stop, please stop," Dr. Bernoune replies. "This is just getting worse. It's harder and harder to believe."

"It's up to you. Take it or leave it. If I went into detail, it would still need belief. I have proof that my story is true. You'll never see Dr. Gorman again and Dad is right here, a witness to the past!"

Dr. Bernoune shakes his head, "No, no." He leaves the tent, still shaking his head. I don't know what else I could have said. Of course, I could have shown him the Sacred Scarab.

"Sorry to change the subject. Darryl, how are you feeling?" Dr. Czerny asks Dad.

"Feeling better by the hour," Dad replies. "Just need a couple of good night's sleep and I'll be much better."

As we're about to leave the mess tent, Dr. Czerny warns us, "Make sure you're ready with information for the next tomb opening tomorrow. I think your introduction to King Djedkare's pyramid complex seemed a bit brief. Probably had other things on your mind."

I finish my coffee, go to my tent, and text Zahra: "Hi. How are you? I'm fine. You said you would like to come see the opening of another tomb. I'm sorry I didn't send this earlier, but we suspended the next opening. We were involved in finding my dad again. He seems to be worse than a teenager. In his defense, he was kidnapped. Anyway, tomorrow would be a good time or later this week if tomorrow is inconvenient."

Her response arrives immediately: "I'll be there tomorrow."

Nathan and I scramble to get our research notes together.

***

At the morning meeting, after working past midnight, I say, "Most of you know us and we hope to give you some background before you start this dig. I'm Jonathan Johnsten."

"I'm Nathan Grant."

"I'd also like to introduce Ms. Zahra Ishmael, a representative of the government," I say, smiling at her. "Dr. Czerny has, to quote him, 'thrown us in at the deep end' to take charge of this excavation. I'm sure the Egyptologists will assist. In 2019, a Czech team was excavating the temple near this pyramid. On that dig, they found a large section of an obelisk."

"Now this was no ordinary obelisk," Nathan says, taking over. "It was an obelisk that recounted the accomplishments of, and I use her titles out of respect, the Great Royal Wife, the God's Wife Setibhor. It also listed her children. The real importance of finding that obelisk is it told us her name for the first time. Lots of reference books still don't list anyone as Djedkare Isisi's wife."

"Dr. Czerny was a very young Egyptologist on that dig," I state, and he laughs. "They had proof then, as we do now, that this is the biggest pyramid complex for a wife of a pharaoh—sorry, king—in the Old Kingdom. Judging by the size of her pyramid and her temple, it is assumed she played a very important role in the life of King Djedkare Isisi, fifth king of the fifth dynasty. She quite possibly assisted him in ascending the throne. Her mortuary temple and the two pyramids are unique."

"If this isn't Sethibhor's pyramid," Nathan continues, "then it could belong to one of the other wives or her daughter: a princess."

"Unfortunately," I add, "this area of the west bank of the Nile is subject to sandstorms from the Sahara and earthquakes."

Suddenly, a squad of soldiers rushes in and stops us. Nathan and I move back from the lectern and our table stacked with handouts. The commanding officer begins yelling at us in Egyptian. Zahra yells back. Abdoullah adds his voice. Then, just as suddenly, the soldiers leave.

"What was that about?" I ask Zahra. I got lost in the Arabic.

"The army is quite nationalist and protective. They thought foreigners were taking over the work here at northern Saqqara."

"I'm glad you and Abdoullah were here. Thanks for telling the Egyptian army we're not the enemy." I turn to address the crew. "Let's try again! So, the Czechs did some work here, but they ran out of time before they could finish examining the pyramid, and it has since become buried. The strength of the Sahara and Saqqara winds have added a great deal of sand over the almost seventy years," I quickly state.

We then head toward the tomb. Fortunately, some of the team have been clearing the sand and Nathan and I organized the setup of winches to move the blocks from in front of the entrance earlier. Our team helps to remove the sand and in about an hour the team operating the winches lifts the last blocks, then we enter the pyramid. Lights are quickly strung to enable us to see inside. Our team is fantastic. We look into the tomb. It is very plain, but beautiful. The ancients used polished limestone blocks to build the walls and ceiling of the entrance. A little farther inside is a serdab with the statue of an imposing woman seated next to a tall man. The woman has a little girl on her knees. I experience the love her parents had, wanting to have this statue of family time with their child made more than four thousand years ago.

"Hey, look at this," Nathan calls, having moved farther along. "Such a wild painted scene."

The walls show a domestic scene of the family; they are seated, and servants carry platters of food. On the wall opposite is a garden with trees, plants, and a pool. There are lots of geese, ducks, and even a stork.

"Okay, Nathan, check this. The stork represents something, but I can't reach it in my brain."

"Perhaps I can help," Zahra smiles. "It looks like a stork, but it is a phoenix, not an actual bird, but a mythological one representing rebirth and eternal life."

"Yeah, got it," I remember. "The Greeks borrowed the phoenix and used it in their mythology, copying it from Egypt. You know, rising from the flames."

Zahra offers an opinion, "The decoration of this area, probably the offering room, was rushed. Just look at the false door. A false door usually has a carved statue of the owner of the tomb. Here, there is no statue, only the hieroglyphs of her name, Kek ret-neb-ti and a small inscription: *ẖkr.t Nb.tj*, 'Jewel of the two beloved,' a testimony to the love in that family."

Dr. Czerny is examining the paintings very closely, "Also, look at this painting. It seems to be unfinished. It's a painting of Princess Kekheretnebti—that's a mouthful. She was the child of King Djedkara Isesi and his wife, Setibhor. We see an image of the princess sitting in a chair, watching wild animals. Now compare the detail in this painting to the one on the other side of the room. They beautifully finished this painting on my right. Green Osiris is sitting on his throne, while the god Anubis weighs Kekheretnehbti's soul against the feather of Maat, truth. So precise. Behind her, we have her mother, Queen Setibhor, watching, and behind the queen, Set with his WAS sceptre."

"Her father, the king," Nathan says smugly, "is not in the painting because King Djedkara Isesi would have to be more than twice the size of any of the other characters. That was the rule.".

We look at the painting, which has great detail. I'm really interested in Set's black jackal head and his bright eyes. He's wearing a white kilt and a gold belt like a king.

My dad, who has joined us, gives us his opinion. "The unfinished painting on the first wall you looked at leads me to the assumption that the death of Kekheretnebti was unexpected."

"I looked her up online. She lived to be about thirty-five years old," Nathan states.

In a very small side room, we find the broken sarcophagus of Kekheretnebti's daughter. I bend down to read the hieroglyphs on the wall over the small sarcophagus. "Her name is Tesit-hor; she died as a young teenager. I don't know about you, but I find this kind of sad and weird," I confess. I feel the scarab come to life. What's going on?

"What's that sound?" Abdoullah whispers. His voice sounds strange, not his usual booming, confident one. Abdoullah seems unsure as to what is happening. I haven't ever seen this.

"It could be the wind blowing over the top of this tomb. The top layers of the pyramid are missing," I suggest, but I sense something mystical might be happening.

The light in the tomb becomes dim as the painting on the wall begins glowing. The room is transforming; it becomes a miraculous sparkling space. It's like being inside a diamond with facets of light shimmering around us. We all gasp for breath. The figures of Anubis, Set, and Setibhor are bright. Without warning, Set and the Great Royal Wife step out of the painting.

Set's menacing jackal face with its long, pointed snout and tall ears frightens me. He speaks in a loud, echoing voice. "Why are you in this sacred place?" he demands. "This is the realm of the daughters of the God-King Djedkare Isesi, Horus on Earth."

Set comes closer. I look at everyone; the god envelopes us completely. Gradually, Set focuses on me, then surrounds me. I'm trying not to shake in his presence. His hollow, loud-sounding voice fills my ears: "Pay respect to Her Majesty."

I'm already bowing. Her majesty waves Set away with the back of her hand. The Great Royal Wife Setibhor moves a few steps towards me and speaks. "I feel a warmth from you. You mean no harm. You wish to ask me something. Tell me what it is."

"It is a great honour for us to be in your daughter's resting place, in your presence.," I say, still bowing. "What I wish to know is, why does this scarab have so much power?" I hold it out to her.

She holds the sacred scarab for several seconds, then says, "This scarab was the property of the magician Ra Nefer Heka. He permeated this scarab with his spiritual powers. It is indeed sacred!" She hands it back to me and puts her hand on my head. I'm filled with a strange energy.

She probes the spirit of each of us. Then she points at Nathan. "Your name means 'given by God.' You and I will meet again." Then she turns, aware of something. I'm not sure what. She looks at Set. A force seems to be coming from her eyes to control him. "Set, do not test my powers. Your evil will have no sway!" she commands.

Set comes threateningly close to me, "You have the sacred scarab, Jonathan." He says my name like it's trash. He then asks for the scarab. I don't know why, but I take it out of my pocket again. He holds it and looks at it carefully. He turns it over, reads it, and then drops it. I catch it, knowing the soapstone could shatter. He reaches out and raises his outstretched arms and hands over my head. Is it a blessing or a curse?

He smiles, baring his sharp teeth. He raises his arm. Even in the tomb, his thunder is deafening. Lightning shoots from his fingers.

Setibhor shouts, “Enough Jackal.”

He moves back to the painting. The tomb grows dark, then lighter, so we can again see the paintings. The Great Royal Wife moves back slightly to welcome King Djedkare. He is majestic. The double white and red crowns of Upper and Lower Egypt are on his head: the uraeus, the gold cobra and vulture gleam. His shoulders are draped with the royal blue sed festival cloak, for he has been king for over thirty years.

We stand silently and I bow appropriately. We don’t grovel like I’m sure his subjects did, but we are very respectful.

“What right have you to be in this sacred space?” he demands. I am suddenly aware that no one else can hear him.

“Your majesty, we are here in the tomb of your daughter by the power of this Sacred Scarab and this ANKH. We respect the sanctity of this tomb. We come from over four thousand years in the future. We have learned of many of your accomplishments: the reform of the administration of your kingdom and your expeditions to Sinai, Punt, Nubia, Lebanon, and Canaan.”

“We are impressed that you know of us, but we have not permitted you to come to our kingdom, to be so familiar with the Great Wife of the God’s body, Setibhor, to enter the tomb of the daughter and the granddaughter of the God’s body.”

It’s taking me a bit of time to translate this in my head and to tell Nathan, Zahra and Abdoullah what the king is saying.

“We know of the maxims of Ptahhotep. His counsel is famous: ‘One knows a wise one because of his wisdom. An official is known by his good deeds: his heart is in balance with his tongue, his lips are accurate when he speaks, in balance with Maat,’” I quote from the world’s first philosopher.

I can see a change on the king’s face. His expression goes from “how dare you,” to “smiling in awareness” to “frustration.”

“Youth,” he finally shouts, “how dare you lecture the king with the axioms of his own scribe!”

I have been told. I translate, but Dr. Czerny and my dad already know what the king said. The rest are silent with the 'What next?' look on their faces.

The Great Royal Wife sees this as her cue. "My royal husband, these visitors from the future do not know of our customs, yet they have been respectful. Indeed, they are knowledgeable, though ignorant. I suggest we send them back to their own time."

"Where are the scarab and ankh you spoke of?" His gaze demands obedience. I produce both.

The king reads the scarab and the hieroglyphs on the handle and frame of the ankh. He looks around; he does not have courtiers, servants, or guards, but he has the gods. I can tell he is calling on all his powers. The king possesses "hu," divine utterance; "sia," divine knowledge; and "heka," divine magic. He clutches his symbols of power, the crook and the flail.

"I call upon you, Thoth, God of Magic, to appear." I feel the ANKH and Sacred Scarab vibrate. The king is commanding all the spirits of Egypt. The light in the tomb changes to a soft violet. Thoth God of Magic, Knowledge and Mysticism is suddenly here. His majestic Ibis mask on his dynamic, muscular body glows. He and the king come sharply into focus.

"Who are these intruders?" the king demands.

We await our fate. Can the spiritual world destroy us mortals?

Thoth divines us. I feel his probing powers. "They are lost 'ka,' souls, your majesty, looking for answers. Do not hamper them. Send them to search for Maat, the love of harmony, in their own time. They have much to learn. This is my knowledge. They have no desire for isfret!"

"We thank you for your wisdom, Thoth," The king replies. Thoth looks directly at the king and then vanishes.

"What is 'isfret?'" Nathan whispers.

"It's chaos," I answer. There is an echo as Zahra, Dad, and Dr. Czerny answer him, too.

With the answer from Thoth, the audience with the king ends. His disappearance dispels the violet light, and Setibhor and Set return to the painting. Setibhor's smile haunts me. Paintings in tombs do not show smiles, just stoic portraits. Yet Setibhor has a slight smile. You can hear everyone finally take a deep breath.

"Jonathan, I certainly think you outdid yourself. A king and queen from the fifth dynasty and two gods," Dad states.

"To tell the truth, I had very little to do with it," I state.

***

Nathan and I walk Zahra to her car.

"Thanks so much for coming. I hope we can—I was going to say do it again, but I think this is a one-time wonder." We all laugh. The tension is gone. We have escaped to reality.

Abdoullah comes up to the parking lot. "Mr. Jonathan, I am still doing the mind is blown. How do you explain?"

"Well, Abdoullah, I can't."

We're all standing around like the party is over, but no one wants to go home. Eventually though, Zahra leaves and the rest of us return to the mess tent where the crew is assembled.

"Now, team, I must thank Jonathan and Nathan for opening and, ah . . . showing us Princess Kekheretnehbti's tomb. So, we all have different versions of this event, I'm sure," Dr. Czerny says.

I says, "As part of this study, we need to document all the paintings on the walls and sift through all the rubble on the floor," I instruct our team workers. Knowing what a leader should say I do, "Nathan and I will work along with you."

So that is how we spend the next week. Dad circulates, taking pictures with the large cameras provided by the international team. We clean the ground, exposing the perfectly cut blocks that make up the floor.

Then, on the weekend, we have a break—a well-earned mental health break. Abdoullah suggests "getting our minds out of the mud." I think it loses something in translation, but it seems right on. He thinks we might like meeting his cousin at the Luxor Museum, but Nathan saw an ad for a hot-air balloon ride. The ride seems more exciting, so we book a trip for the next morning.

The staff for the balloons look smart in their white shirts and black ties. The two brightly coloured balloons are bobbing on their anchors. Once everyone has been checked in, we climb aboard, the jets of hot air are fired, and the balloons fill as we sail up into the wild blue. I look at Abdoullah. He's looking very pale. This is not his idea of fun. We should have checked.

The trip takes us high over the Temples of Karnak and Luxor, heads west over the Nile, and then over Medinet Habu, the temple of Ramses the III. Next, we sail south over Hatshepsut's classic temple.

Suddenly, a strong wind picks up and the balloon begins rising and then falling without notice. Abdullah loses his breakfast over the side of the basket. The captain is trying to control the balloon, but if he cuts the jet of hot air to try and lose altitude, he has less control of the direction the balloon is headed. He fires the gas jets again. Then we start moving sideways and swaying wildly. I look at Nathan.

"I had no idea it would be like this!" he yells.

We begin moving north back down the Nile. The wind dies down a bit and we stop bobbing. Finally, the wind cooperates, and the balloon is directed back to a field near Luxor where we bounce along before losing enough hot air to land. Abdoullah is glad it's over. When he gets out of the basket, he falls to the ground and kisses it. We're all glad to be on solid ground, but not to the same extent.

"I should have let you know I am not the friend of high things," Abdoullah says.

"Yes, but you did it. You conquered your fear!" I exclaim. He could have complained, but he didn't.

I'm half joking but going up that high and being caught in a windstorm is not everyone's idea of fun. I look around. Sure enough, there is Set hiding among the clouds. I think I can hear him laughing. I turn around and see Abdoullah and Nathan staring at me.

CHAPTER EIGHT

ABDOULLAH TELLS HIS PROBLEM

When the bus stops, Abdoullah and I jump off and walk the few blocks to his mother's apartment.

"Abdoullah, why did we take the city bus to your mother's apartment?" I ask.

"The street is in an old section of Cairo. Always has too many cars parked or left along the street. There is barely enough room for a car to get through. If we came in a vehicle, we would have to walk blocks and that takes time. The bus stops at the end of my mother's street."

The old block building is crumbling in places. Laundry hangs from the balconies and trees have become overgrown. The nearby minaret has the call to prayer going full blast. The pleasant ancient call that used to be sung has been replaced by a recording and a loudspeaker. The pavement on the street is cracked and even missing in some places, replaced by pools of stagnant water. Abdoullah looks at the building. This used to be his home. Twenty years have passed. It is old, dirty, and uncared for. He opens the gate to the square in front of the building.

We hurry up the stairs and Abdoullah opens the door to the apartment. His mother is sitting, holding her apron up to her eyes. Her once black hair is now streaked with white and her face and neck have become wrinkled. Abdoullah's oldest brother, Basra, looks up when we come in.

"Ah, the traitor, working for the white foreigners."

"Good to see you too, Basra. Where is Fatma?" Abdoullah demands.

"What's it to you?"

"I was nearby and thought I'd drop in," Abdoullah says.

"You brought this American with you? Well, you are too late. She's getting married."

"I wasn't invited?" Abdoullah feigns being hurt.

"Haven't you got it? You are not wanted here." I get the idea that Basra is jealous of Fatma and Abdoullah's close relationship.

"Okay, Basra, she phoned me. Asked me to come."

Basra runs at him. I'm stunned. "Stay out of our lives!" he shouts. He pushes Abdoullah, almost knocking him over, then he punches him. Abdoullah fights back.

Their mother shrieks. "No, No!"

Basra doesn't care. He tries to knock Abdoullah out with the leg of a broken chair, but Abdoullah dodges his blow and punches low. Basra doubles over. Then Abdoullah gives him a double-fisted blow to the head. He's down. I can see that Abdoullah feels sorry, but obviously Basra did not want to talk this out.

"Mother, where is Fatma?" Abdoullah asks.

"At the house of your uncle, Saleem. He wants to marry Fatma to his wife's old nephew. 225 Tent Sewers Street."

We go out to the street. "We need backup," Abdoullah says as he phones Jabari. "Jabari, I need help. Tent Sewers Street."

"On my way, Abdoullah." He speaks so clearly; I can hear him.

We get to Abdoullah's uncle's apartment and stand outside. "We'll wait a few minutes and Jabari will be here," Abdoullah says, but we don't have to wait.

"I came right away," Jabari says as he runs up the street.

"Thanks," Abdoullah says. We clap each other on the back. "My sister has been abducted by my uncle to marry her off to some old relative of his. I want to go in and get her out."

"Where is she?"

"This is the building. 225 Tent Sewers."

We head inside without knocking, but it seems we won't be noticed. Abdoullah's uncle's apartment is large and many people are crammed into the living space. We see Fatma, dressed as a bride, and push through to her.

Abdoullah gets right to the point. "Fatma, do you want to marry this man?"

"No, Abdoullah," Fatma shrieks defiantly. "I do not. No!"

Abdoullah takes one of her arms and I take the other.

Jabari shouts, "I dare anyone to stop us."

Before their uncle knows what is happening, we're gone. As we run down the street, Fatma laughs and throws off the elaborately embroidered headscarf she was forced to wear. I grab it. She can sell it.

We get to a liberal cafe where men and women can be together. People look at her dress questioningly.

"What am I going to do, Jonathan? I need to have a safe place for my sister. I can't take her back to my mother's house. My older brother wants this to happen, and he wants to have a fight with me over this."

"I'll phone the camp," I say. "I'm sure Dr. Czerny or my dad will take Fatma in and give her a job. They hire many locals to work in the kitchen or the laundry. I'll phone. Wait just a minute." I step out of the café and watch Abdoullah and Fatima through the window.

Abdoullah looks across the table at his sister. Her eyes have too much makeup and her lips are bright red, but despite that, she's a beautiful young woman. I know she's bright and could have a career if given a chance, or education and training. Then she could be whatever she wants to be.

"Good news," I say when I come back, "they're glad to help. We can take her with us back to the dig. She'll be safe there."

The four of us go over to Abdoullah's mother's apartment to pack a bag. Basra yells at us as soon as we step in the door. "What are you doing? Abdoullah? It is all arranged. We don't want you here."

"Who besides you wants this marriage for her?" Abdoullah challenges.

Their mother comes into the central room. Her mother calls Fatma by her family's pet name. "Oh, my Fifi, I am so glad you are safe."

"I have got her work at the camp where I work. She will be safe there. Basra, I will get the police if you try anything. Women are free in Egypt. Wake up. Things have changed."

Fatma quickly packs her things and hugs her mother goodbye. As we leave, Abdoullah says, "I am so glad to get out of here. It is a place many years behind most of Egypt."

Jabari carries one of Fatma's bags as we get onto a city bus. We meet up with a van from camp at the bus terminal. When we get in, Fatma starts crying.

"Are you so sad to be leaving mother?" Abdoullah asks.

Fatma shakes her head and smiles with tears on her cheeks, makeup running down. "I am crying because I am happy; I am crying because I am free!"

"Jabari, thank you for being my support. We couldn't have saved her without you," Abdoullah says.

Jabbari waves goodbye as he walks down the street. This tall thin man in the worn Jellabiya is a real friend.

When we arrive back at camp, Dr. Czerny comes out to the van.

"This my sister, Fatma," Abdoullah introduces. "She is looking like too much makeup because of the wedding that we stopped.

"They are expecting Fatma in the kitchen," Dr. Czerny says.

Thankfully, Abdoullah says, "I will take her to my tent so she can wash and change and then take her to the kitchen where she can work."

As we're walking to our tents, Abdoullah turns to me. "Jonathan. I can't say anything." He just hugs me and whispers, "Thank you."

CHAPTER NINE
ABDOULLAH & SALEEM

Abdoullah has not heard from his mother. She doesn't like him phoning and talking to her because Basra gets angry. Her youngest son, Lateef, would like for Basra to show respect for their mother. Sometimes Basra hits Lateef hard and threatens our mother.

It all seems like chaos from what Abdoullah tells me. Abdoullah needs to know what's going on, so he phones. I stand next to the phone so I can hear.

"Ah, Abdoullah, you phone me. You must have known to talk to me. Basra is so angry about Fatma going with you to work for the foreigners. He won't help with any money but expects me to feed him."

"What about Lateef? Doesn't he get paid for his work?"

"He is a taxi driver so doesn't always make much. Must pay the taxi company more and more. If he has tips, that is great. But he is still in school. He's a bright boy. He should get an education. I tell him, 'Hide yourself in your books,' but he doesn't like being home with Basra yelling at him and pushing him around, so sometimes he goes to the awah."

"You check your bank account?" Abdoullah asks. I look at him and mouth, "Why are you asking this?"

"Yes, the same for a long time."

"Good. I'll start sending you more money. Tell Basra to pay his share or I will talk to the Mullah at our mosque. What about uncle, Saleem? Is he still a troublemaker?"

"Saleem is trying to get Basra to work with him. They will go looking for graves to rob near Giza, I think. He is bound for jail, I tell him."

"I will come see you soon, Uum." He uses the word Egyptians call their mother.

I sit down with Abdoullah for a minute and get a cup of coffee. "Abdoullah, why do you speak English to your mother?"

"I do this because she is educated and knows some English, but Basra doesn't know much and can't understand us. Basra is going to get into trouble. Such a worry for my mother. If they don't catch him for digging into tombs, they will get him for selling what he finds. I know Basra. If he finds something worth anything, he will brag about it and the police will hear about this and catch him."

"Let's have a chat with Dr. Czerny or Dad and ask for their advice."

We find them at camp, sitting outside in the shade of a tree. "Excuse me," Abdoullah says, "I am having a problem."

Dad turns towards me, but asks, "What is it, Abdoullah?"

"My brother is a guy who wants to get rich without working for it.

He is organizing a gang to go to Giza, near the Red Pyramid at Dahshur, and rob some tombs. My mother says he has become a bully. Gives my younger brother a rough time. Slaps him around. I need some help. He can't rob tombs; the police will get him."

"I think, Abdoullah, you were right in telling us about this," Dad says. "But, Jonathan, you and Nathan are better at being detectives and finding solutions than I am. Why don't you look into this and see how we can help? We can give you time off."

Abdoullah and I find Nathan. After learning about the situation, Nathan is not so keen to help.

"I don't want to go out riding over the sand dunes, being a perfect target for some tomb robbers," he complains.

"I'm doing this for Abdoullah. His brother Basra is off the rails, looking for a mastaba, a bench shaped kind of tomb often lost in sand. He and his partners look for such a tomb and will rob it. Abdoullah knows the police watch the area around the pyramids for vandals and robbers."

"Not a great use of our time," Nathan states.

"Your choice," I say. "So, Abdoullah, do you think Basra is crazy enough to rob a tomb or mastaba? What do you think he will do?" I ask.

"I am told Basra will go to the plain of Dahshur, near the Red Pyramid, and find a mastaba that looks undisturbed, like it has not been excavated. They will probably go after sundown."

"I want to know more about the Red Pyramid. What do you know about it, Abdoullah?"

"Not much. I know it was built by King Sneferu. He is the one who built this one, the Red Pyramid, the first true pyramid. It was his third try. The fine white limestone on the front of it was stolen, so only the red granite is left."

"That's right. I remember that's how it got its name," I say. "I suggest we go out there tonight as soon as it gets dark. We'll be able to see for kilometres across the plain." I add, "Are you in, Nathan?"

"What the hell! I have nothing to lose, I hope."

We drive out there, park and wait.

"Well, this is not working," Abdoullah says. "I'm eager to catch my brother before something illegal happens."

"Patience, Abdoullah," I say just as we see a pickup driving across the plain. We jump from the jeep and start walking towards the pickup's lights. I have a large flashlight. When we get to the guys who rode the pickup, they are excavating what they hope is a mastaba or ruined pyramid that has been covered by sand. I shine my light on them. They drop their shovels and run to their truck.

"No, Basra is not one of them," Abdoullah tells us. We go back to the jeep where we wait for another hour.

"I think we should go back to camp," I suggest.

"I have a hunch," Nathan says. "Give it ten more minutes." As he finishes speaking, a truck drives across the plain from the south. A man gets out.

Abdoullah says, "I recognize the swagger walk."

Two more men get out of the truck and look around. They find a mound of sand and set up lanterns at their chosen site.

"I think you've changed our luck, Nathan," I chuckle.

"Let's sneak up on them," Nathan says.

We get in close and I shine my flashlight in their faces.

"What are you doing? Robbing graves?" Abdoullah shouts in Arabic.

One man pulls a gun and shoots at us. We hit the ground. Nathan takes his gun out and fires back.

Abdoullah shouts, "We have the police coming." He does.

The gunman shoots again. Nathan fires back again. Then one man screams and the other three men run for it.

I run over to the wounded man. Abdoullah is right behind me.

"It's my brother!" he says. Of course, it is.

"I thought I was shooting over their heads," Nathan mumbles. "Sorry."

***

At the hospital, we have to fill in a police report for a shooting. Abdoullah doesn't know what to say. Basra's shirt is soaked with blood.

"I suggest you tell the truth. Just say, 'We work for Egyptologists and had a report of tomb robbers.' Then ask, 'how would the police like to handle this?'" I say.

The hospital treats this all like a routine thing. Basra just has a bullet in the shoulder.

After the hospital releases him, we take Basra home. Abdoullah and I help him up the stairs. He seems weak. I think he lost quite a lot of blood.

Abdoullah's mother is in a panic when she sees Basra bandaged. She tries to hug him while Abdoullah and I try to keep his arm elevated. I'm sure it would look hilarious if you weren't involved. Basra's mother's tears for her wounded son, whom she was ready to kick out of the house, are intense and a bit melodramatic. We finally untangle them and get him lying down on the sofa in their living room.

"You shot your own brother?" his mother says to Abdoullah.

"It was an accident. It was Nathan that shot the gun."

"What were you doing, Basra, to get the nice Canadian man to shoot you?"

She's too emotional, so I take over. "Okay, Basra, why were you digging at Dahshur? Did you have some information about a tomb or mastaba?" I want to know, but he refuses to speak. I would like to give his injured arm a yank. I restrain myself, but maybe he senses our frustration with the scene.

Finally, Basra answers, but keeps his eyes lowered. I think he feels like a loser. "I was at the awah. A guy there said he had heard an Egyptologist from the National Museum talking on TV, that some mastabas have never been excavated. He talked about knowing where some are. I think we found something."

"That information is true," I say. "I just wish we had more to go on."

Abdoullah sits next to his brother. "Do you really think there is something there? Did you find some of the mud bricks of the mastaba under the sand?"

Basra doesn't talk.

"Listen, Basra, Jonathan's father might help us get a permit, make it legal, and then we will get paid for recovering objects from the tomb," Abdoullah pushes.

At the mention of getting paid, Basra looks up.

"If we get permission for an exploration of a mastaba, would you like to be part of the team?" I ask.

"I think this might mean Basra can get his head straightened," Abdoullah whispers to me.

"Let us talk to our Egyptologists," Nathan suggests. "Might as well get something out of this mess."

We leave Basra at home and head out.

***

We are all ready for a good night's sleep, even though the sky is starting to show the first light of dawn. When we drive into camp, Dad comes running out in his pajama pants.

"Sorry to wake you, sir," Nathan says.

"I had a restless night. I want to know how your stakeout went," Dad replies.

"We got shot at by some tomb robbers, then Nathan shot back and winged a guy who turned out to be Abdoullah's brother, Basra. Basra thinks they found something in that mound," I tell him. "It's probably a mastaba."

"I guess it could have been worse," Dad states. He continues, "I think there are some steps to this excavation. First, you three need to get some sleep. Then you need to have brunch or whatever you want to call it. Third, bring Basra out here so we can get some information from him and see if there really is a mastaba out there that we can investigate."

Since his plan is logical, and we're all so tired, we follow it. When we finally sleep eat and bring Basra to camp, he isn't quite sure about all of us, but we get him to relax and "spill the beans," as they say. Abdoullah of course wants to know what beans.

CHAPTER TEN
JONATHAN LEADS A TEAM

Dad and Dr. Czerny get behind the plan to help Abdoullah by helping Basra. Abdoullah has really become a part of our excavation family.

I find Abdoullah in his tent reading the Cairo news. "I'm not feeling confident about this," I tell him. "I really want to help Basra, but I'm concerned. He has lived a life on the edge. He might not really have changed. He might be tempted to take some items and sell them on the black market. He might tell some of his former friends of the results of our dig," I confess.

"He did the change very quick. You and I will keep the eyes on him," Abdoullah confirms.

After brunch, I stick my head in the kitchen and see Fatma busily washing pots and pans. "How are you liking your new job?" I ask.

"I am happy, so happy," she says and smiles. She is not only enjoying her job but learning some English.

It takes a full week to hear back from the Department of Antiquities because of other permits and government projects. Finally, we get a permit for the mastaba that Basra located, but it has stipulations. The

Czech Institute is working in Abousir and Dr. Michal Bakry will join us. Surprisingly, he is blond and blue-eyed like Nathan, except he's shorter and has wide shoulders. He looks like he's ready to take on the job at hand.

I sit down at a table in camp with Dr. Bakry and the designated team. We'll all be working together: Nathan, Abdoullah, Basra, Jabari, and me. We try to put together all that is known of the mastaba at Dahshur. Dad and Dr. Bakry have a wealth of knowledge about Amenemhet II, whose tomb is also at Dahshur. The two Egyptologists give us the background of the many tombs in Dahshur.

Dad and Dr. Bakry give us a lot of background information from their work on the twelfth dynasty.

"Located close to the pyramid of King Amenemhet II of the Twelfth Dynasty," Dad begins, "several tombs of the Princesses Ita, Itaweret, and Khenmet were found untouched, still containing their beautiful jewels, and also the tombs of the Lady Sathathormeryt. Their jewellery has been determined to be of the highest stage of metalworking in Egypt during this time period. There are also several tombs of nobles buried here. The princes' tombs have not all been found. It is possible to say that there are mastabas in Dahshur that have not been excavated, but there are also tombs that have been robbed. I would say it is a gamble."

"Perhaps with the story you have, Basra, we can find a mastaba that has survived robbing," I state taking on the leadership role.

We set off to Dahshur and, following Basra's lead, we come to an enormous pile of sand, perhaps the indication of a mastaba.

In a loud voice, I instruct the men from camp, "We need to start moving the sand from the north end of this mastaba. This is where the entrance to a tomb may be."

The team digs in with lots of help from us. It's great to see Basra and Abdoullah working together and chatting.

"Come on, Basra, you can move more sand than that!" Abdoullah shouts.

Basra replies, "Mother made me the strongest child. Try to keep up, little brother."

This results in laughter from all of us because Basra is much shorter than Abdoullah. The common goal is bringing them together.

Since most tombs were built with the entrance on the north end, that's where we focus our efforts. Success! Moving sand from that end exposes the entrance.

"Jonathan, look at this," my father calls. I always thought a mastaba was a small tomb. Wrong. They can be quite large, I realize.

"Can you read these hieroglyphs?" Dad asks me. There is a large pillar at the entrance to the tomb.

"Ptahshepses favoured by His Majesty, King Niuserre, Life, Prosperity, Health," I read.

We keep working until our work pays off and we excavate the central court of the tomb. It has five beautiful columns. It's surprising that the ancient Egyptians, who had rigid restrictions about how paintings had to be done, were not rigid about pillars. These round columns were painted a deep blue and have white and gold capitals.

"This certainly is worth finding," I exclaim.

"But no treasure," Basra states.

"We have more work to go yet," Abdoullah says, encouraging him.

We all pitch in and continue to uncover more of the court and then rooms that open from it.

Dad soon suggests we stop. "We're all tired and need a well-deserved supper, and then we can start fresh in the morning."

The camp has been well staffed, and Mudads, the camp's chef, calls us to the mess tent soon after we have time to wash up. "It is a good name for a cook, Mudads. It means 'the provider,'" Abdoullah says.

"Well, thanks for that, Abdoullah," I say.

We have just started our meal when we hear shouting in the kitchen. A couple of us get up and to find out what's happening when a gang of men, their faces covered, enter the tent with guns pointed at us.

"Sit," one of them yells in English. "Show us your treasures," he continues.

"You're out of luck," Basra yells at them in Egyptian. "We have found no treasure. The police are coming. We have good security. So go."

A young guy from the kitchen staff rushes in and grabs the leader's gun, which shoots up in the air, but another gunman shoots at us. I feel pain in my hip and fall to the ground.

A silvery grey cloud fills the tent and Set appears shooting lightning into the air across the huge tent and laughing at the chaos. Before we can react, Khepri emerges from His misty purple cloud and points His WAS sceptre, first at Set, who shrinks, and then at each of the gunmen, who fall to the ground.

A few minutes later, the police arrive. They wonder why they have been called. I hear the ambulance screaming its way from Cairo before blacking out.

I come to in a hospital room to find my clothes gone. A gown just covers my shoulders and chest. I go to pull it down but realize there is a doctor extracting a bullet from my hip.

Seeing me awake, he says, "I have given you a local anesthetic and a sleeping pill. I've got it," he says holding up the bullet. Now all you need to do is heal. We'll take care of the infection. Everyone is all right. Unfortunately, the young man, I think he was from the kitchen staff, was killed."

I wish he hadn't rushed in. I think we were almost to the point where the gunmen realized there was no treasure to be had. Guns. I don't like them.

I doze, and when I wake, there is a sense of comfort—my pain is leaving. How is this happening? I look around my room. Everything has a purple glow and then I realize I'm in a purple mist.

I see Khepri. "You attract danger. You are fortunate I am indeed your protector!"

He points his WAS sceptre at me, and my hip completely heals. I bow towards Khepri as another miracle occurs and he vanishes. I wish I could explain it properly. When I see him, it's as if particles come together and then he is there. When he leaves, it's as if the visual part of him slowly becomes mist.

I walk out of the hospital, even though they have a wheelchair rule for patients when they leave. Back at camp, I'm ready for lunch. I walk into the mess tent. Everyone from our team is there. They're glad to see me. "Look at you, Jono, always beating the odds. You're supposed to be laid up for two weeks," Nathan shouts.

I head for the food laden counter and pile a plate with salad, veggies, and some meat casserole. It looks so good.

After lunch, we all head back to Dahshur in a couple of jeeps. We unlock the barrier set in front of the entrance by security and go through the first corridor, then the hall of columns before being confronted by a wall. I sort of huddle with Dad and Dr. Czerny, hoping we can come up with an answer for this.

"I think the builders would have wanted to ensure robbers didn't keep going straight, so to trick them, they created turns to the left or right. Let's divide into two teams and investigate the side walls here at the end of this room," Dad says.

Soon, the group on the left yells out, "We found something." We join them and we can see there are different colours in the blocks and clay on one side. We set to work breaking down the entrance to the next section. Some of us work on the wall and some of us haul the blocks and bags of clay out of the tomb. The hall is just a long corridor with no plaster, paintings, or granite slabs to provide a beautiful surface. At the end, when we're about to give up, we find a surprising room. The walls are plastered and painted with *The Book of Coming Forth by Day*, a very important section of *The Book of the Dead.*

"This is wonderful," Dr. Czerny says. "All this colour, this is remarkable. I will translate the hieroglyphs.

"A Hymn of Praise to RA When He Riseth in the Eastern Part of Heaven. Behold Osiris, Qenna the merchant, triumphant, who saith: 'Homage to thee, O thou who risest in Nu, and who at thy manifestation dost make the world bright with light; the whole company of gods sing hymns of praise unto thee after thou hast come forth.' The divine Mertir who minister unto thee cherish thee as King of the north and south, thou beautiful and beloved Man-child. When thou risest, men and women live. The nations rejoice in thee, and the souls of Annu sing unto thee songs of joy. The souls of the cities of Pe and Nekhen exalt thee, the apes of dawn adore thee, and all beasts and cattle praise thee with one accord.

"Well, you get the sense of the book," Dr. Czerny finishes. " It is fascinating this section is copied here. Today, you can find it online or buy a hard copy. The original is in the museum in Leiden, Germany. My eyes get tired quickly. We should have Zahra with her young eyes here."

The hieroglyphs are written as a decoration as well as the spell for the Ka to follow to the Field of reeds.

In this room decorated with hieroglyphs is the sarcophagus. I kneel down and read out the hieroglyphs, which spell the name Prince Isesi-Ankh.

Dr. Czerny and Dad both look stunned. "This can't be," Dad says. "The mastaba of Isesi-Ankh was discovered in Saqqara south. But other than some broken pottery, the tomb was empty, robbed."

"Sorry, Basra. No gold," Abdoullah says.

"Ah," Basra responds, "but look, such beautiful pictures and hieroglyphs." The man has been reformed. A minor miracle.

Our work in the mastaba done, we go back to the mess tent where coffee is always ready. Today, the cook Mudads has baked cinnamon buns. "I heard that you westerners like these buns, so I try to bake them," Mudads says. He smiles and is delighted that we like them.

Dr. Czerny is not as much a westerner as we are, but he is enjoying a bun with his coffee. "Before we were interrupted by Basra and the search for a mastaba at Dahshur, we were working on Ptahshepses' tomb. It is still waiting for us," he states. "So, tomorrow morning, back to Ptahshepses' tomb."

The next morning, the guys and I head over to the admin tent. Dr. Bakry is ready for us. "When Ptahshepses' tomb was discovered, we found his sarcophagus in a small room. According to plans used in many tombs, I think there are other small rooms off this central court. There may be some architraves over the rooms, so I think we can find rooms under each one."

Both Nathan and Abdoullah are looking at me for a definition. "Okay, an architrave is the long stone that runs above a doorway. It's supported by pillars on each side of the entrance to a room in a tomb." Relief. Smiles. "So, we take away the sand and debris high up in the tomb. Then under each architrave, we search for a door to find the room that were used for Ptahshepses' sarcophagus and rooms for his furniture and chests of goods he would like to have in the afterlife," I say.

We all set to work, and after two days, we find what we've been looking for. The next day, we excavate the rooms. In one is the sarcophagus of Ptahshepses' wife, Keminab, and in the other, his second son, Amenemhatankh. These carved stone sarcophagi are beautiful, but not as extravagant as the gold-covered coffins inside. The tomb of Amenemhatankh had been used by another member of a succeeding royal family. They had stolen the false door with its fantastic frame and used it in another tomb. Weird.

The next room is a surprise. It contains wonderful statues of the gods and chests of jewellery of the Great Royal Wife. There are statues of Ptah of course; Isis, goddess of love; Bes, god of music, childbirth, merriment and protector of children; Taweret the hippopotamus goddess of the Nile, and Thoth, god of education and knowledge. We laugh at Bes' squat figure. Basra's eyes widen with excitement. "I told you there was gold in Abousir!" he exclaims.

Basra got a good-sized cheque for his efforts. He realizes there are rewards for being honest. Our work is done once the tomb is cleaned and turned over to the government.

Nathan and I decide to be ordinary tourists for a while and visit Karnak and Giza. To make it more fun, we ask Zahra if she would like to join us on a cheap river cruise. So, in a few days, we jovially board a felucca—an open boat powered by a huge sail and the winds that blow up the Nile. We see the temples at Edfu, Abydos, and Kom Ombo. At Kom Ombo we see a beautiful carving, a scarab with two crocodiles, Sobek, above it.

At night, the tour's crew puts up tents. We sit around the fire as they serenade us with songs in Egyptian. Because I have a beard coming in, I think they're probably making me the joke of their song by referring to me as "Monsieur Moustache." I wish Abdoullah was here so I could get a translation.

It's so relaxing to just sit on board and enjoy the tranquil lapping of the river against the boat. Of course, we bring along our own curse. On the final day of our trip, the wind picks up and starts blowing us back and forth across the river. We offer to leave so their boat is not wrecked. We're able to get back up north by train.

CHAPTER ELEVEN

KHENTKAUS' CURSED TOMB

Dr. Czerny, his eyes twinkling and his smile relaxing, organizes all of us to be at the opening of our last project of the season. He puts Nathan and me on the staff roster to present the research for this next site.

"Nathan and Jonathan impressed me with the research done on the last tomb, so as this is our last of the season, I have asked them to do it again, maybe with less dazzle," he chuckles.

Dr. Czerny leaves us to it.

"Thank you, Dr. Czerny," Nathan begins. "We're excited to be starting our excavation of the pyramid of the fifth dynasty's Great Royal Wife Khentkaus II. She was the wife of Neferirkare Kakai and the mother of two kings."

"Thanks, Nathan," I say, taking over. "We're lucky to have a keen Egyptian history lover, Zahra Ishmahel, with us again. I don't have a lot to tell you because this tomb is a mystery. Her pyramid is larger than those of many other wives of pharaohs. She was also possibly a regent for one of her sons. The locals believe her pyramid is cursed, so we will be careful." This brought some laughter. After the presentation, we head to the dig site.

We all look in distress at the immense pile of sand that was Khentkaus II's mastaba.

"I know I spoke of a pyramid, but it's probably a mastaba," I tell the team.

"I hope mastaba doesn't mean a pile of sand," Nathan says, laughing at his own joke. "I know the word 'mastaba' is really Arabic for bench, because that's the shape of these tombs."

Abdoullah joins in with a clever remark. "I asked Allah to bless us, but I did not think he would bless us with so much sand."

"I'm glad our friend still has a sense of humour," I say. I put my notes in my trusty backpack, then we all put on headbands with lights.

We start with laughter, and by noon, we are groaning, but we've uncovered one end of the mastaba. Fortunately, Nathan and I had checked the site out earlier and found out which end of the mastaba has the entrance. Unfortunately, stones, discarded mud bricks, and drifted sand have blocked our way, but we soon make a good start on uncovering the opening. After Dr. Czerny, the four of us, Abdoullah, Zahra, Nathan, and I, enter first, walking on the smooth floor in the opening passage. I feel excited. There's a smile on my face as we're all fascinated by the polished, subtle sheen on the walls. Soon the tomb is illuminated by two dramatically large paintings of the Great Royal Wife Khentkaus. She is pictured in her garden, and behind her in both paintings is a young, stereotypical man. The hieroglyphs down the sides and bottom list the amazing qualities of Khentkaus and mention the man as her most loyal architect.

Zahra is just a few steps in front of me when, without warning, a trap set to catch robbers opens. Slabs of floor fall. Zahra shouts as she falls to another level of the tomb. She is now in what the Czech team had decided is a chapel. I'm not sure how they accessed it. We all go to her rescue, but Abdoullah jumps down and gets to her first.

"Are you all right, Miss Zahra?" Abdoullah asks, lifting her up by the elbow.

"Just surprised. I didn't expect the drop," she laughs. The laugh proves she isn't hurt. What I'm wondering is, why didn't the trap work when the Czech team entered the tomb?

When we get down to the lower level, we discover stairs down to another room below the "chapel."

"I think we need to remove more flooring so we can get access," Nathan suggests.

"Before anything more happens, what is the curse of the Great Royal Wife Khentkaus, the wife of Neferirkare Kakai?" Dad asks.

I think I surprise him by knowing a viable answer. "She is said to be Mut-nesut-bity-nesut-bity, 'Mother of Two Kings of Upper and Lower Egypt' or more controversially, 'Mother of the King of Upper and Lower Egypt, and King of Upper and Lower Egypt.'

"Writers say it was a curse because her first-born son, Neferefre, was king only a few years; her second son, Shepseskare, lived only a few months as an adult and may never have been king; and finally, her third son, Nyuserre Ini, escaped the curse and lived twenty-four to thirty-five years. There is more to this curse. I have heard from locals working on this tomb that one of the Czech team was killed here. That's why they didn't finish excavating the tomb. They abandoned the project."

Dr. Czerny says, "The death is not in their published notes of the work done here. I wonder why? They must have had to report it. Police? Hospital? Maybe it didn't happen."

We're all quiet. Nathan breaks the silence. "There is another curse. Over centuries, there have been torrential rains and at least one earthquake, filling this lower chamber with debris and mud."

"I think the mud and sand have become the next best thing to sedimentary rock!" Zahra, who is working on excavating the exposed room, suggests, and we laugh, but it's true.

We keep working on the rubble, hauling out bucketful after bucketful.

"Hey, look at this," I say, pointing. "I can see more of the floor. There is hope!"

We work for several more hours. I can see Zahra using a brush and working carefully. Of course, I enjoy watching Zahra any time. I sense she can see something of value because she switched from trowel to brush to avoid damaging it.

"What did you find?" I ask.

"I'm not sure, but I can see part of a statue."

All the men start working carefully in pairs. The ancient Egyptians carefully planned and hid the true chapel and its gods. Soon, as we work with trowels and brushes, we uncover statues, some broken and some complete. Khnum, the ram-headed god, is found. We also find Atum, the creator, and a broken one of Horus. We find broken baskets that still have some grain remaining in them, offerings to the gods. There are also a few items of jewellery, mainly bracelets and gold chains. I'm surprised at how great the find is, and the Egyptologists are as well.

Nathan comes over to me and whispers, "Look at this." He has a beautiful pectoral pendant. You know where pecs are from the gym, so this sits on a person's chest. It is the eye of Horus, made of gold and lapis lazuli. The frame for the eye is a crowned winged vulture on the left and a crowned cobra on the right. Coloured faience and gemstone beads form the chain. "I'm going to wear it today for good luck." He tucks it inside his shirt.

"Don't get too attached to it. We should hand it over for cataloguing. Don't forget to do that," I say, trying to be stern. We should be able to enjoy our work.

The Czech team had declared this tomb of Khentkaus excavated and catalogued in 1980, but they also stated they ran out of time. Fortunately, we have lots of canvas bags available for rubble and sand. We continue working in the lower level and eventually work our way to a new space. It's much larger than expected. It's a tunnel-like room that stretches for many metres under the plateau. The secrets of Saqqara are amazing.

Zahra and I set up a sieve and screen the material from the new room.

"Jonathan, look at these," Zahra says. "Under a coat of mud, I found two small but beautiful statues, statues carved from alabaster."

"They're awesome! So much detail. It's Isis. Look at the exquisite detail of her face, the realistic braiding of her wig!" I explode in admiration. The second is her sister Nephthys. Though small this statue had an enigmatic smile as if the goddess knew something.

One of our team members unearths some incredible statues of a family: children of different ages and their parents. "These latest finds suggest we need to use brushes to avoid damaging the artefacts buried in the compact material," I suggest.

We continue to work in the congealed mud and, gradually, an entire group of gods and goddesses made of gold, silver, and electrum come to light.

We soon see that the walls of the chapel are covered in paintings of the Great Royal Wife sitting in a garden with her children. "This painting is the same as Khentkaus' chapel in Memphis," Dad states. "It has been recreated here as part of her tomb." He continues working next to Nathan and me.

"Ah, here he is," Nathan calls out. "Set, who sought me out in Vancouver." He holds up a beautiful gold statue of the jackal-headed god. As he says this, thunder cracks over our heads. Lightning flashes even in the depths of this tomb, and Nathan drops the statue. A dark storm cloud fills the space and soon Set stands in the tomb.

"Do not mock me, mortal!" Set says, raising his WAS sceptre. Lightning forks across the ceiling. We hear a rumbling from deep in the earth. The walls of the tomb shift and fall. Earthquake!

Zahra and I look at each other with intense fear. The earth shakes again, and I fall farther into the bottom of the tomb. The floor of the tomb shifts and traps me with Nathan and Dad. We wait until there is silence.

Dad and I begin digging towards what we hope is a way out, but we're running out of air. Nathan just lies on the floor of the tomb, a slab of stone beside him. The light on my headgear is fading but Dad and I keep digging upwards. Then we hear muffled voices, but there's even less air now and Dad's light goes out.

Finally, a hole! We make it larger so Dad can climb out. I notice Dad has something clutched in his hand: a gold statue of King Neferirkare Kakai. He rescued it when he began crawling out, a dedicated Egyptologist.

"I need help!" I shout. I look up between the fallen blocks of the tomb and see Abdoullah's hand reach down; his strength helps pull me out.

Suddenly, the earth shakes again. Aftershock! The vast blocks of the roof of the tomb shift again. I hear a scream, which rings in the ancient tomb. I will never forget it. It's the only time I've heard Nathan scream like that.

Hydraulics on site begin lifting enormous blocks but it takes so long. Zahra stands beside me and holds my hand. "They'll never get him out in time," I say.

Finally, the hydraulic team gets to Nathan. I jump back between the fallen blocks into the dark tomb. Zahra yells, "Jonathan, don't!"

Team members try to help me lift Nathan. He is so limp. Blood is running from an open wound on the side of his face. The space between the blocks is too small to carry him out. I suddenly realize what I must do.

I hold onto the scarab and Nathan's hand. Lights flash, then the space becomes dark. Light flashes brightly again, and we're turning and turning. It seems to take too long.

Now Nathan lies at my feet in an empty space in the tomb. Where are we? I see a wonderful pale pink light shining around us. The tomb is no longer wrecked, but under construction. A woman, regally dressed, appears. There is a splendid golden diadem around the wig on her head with five gold ribbons cascading down the back. I recognize the Great Royal Wife Setibhor.

She looks at Nathan lying dead at my feet. She bends and takes his hand. Setibhor smiles her enigmatic smile at Nathan. "I sensed we would meet again."

Setibhor passes me her WAS staff. She holds out her hands as if in blessing. I instinctively give her the Sacred Scarab. She holds the Eye of Horus inside Nathan's shirt. She has her right hand on the Eye of Horus and the other on the scarab.

I instinctively know what I am to do. I grab a "Book of Spells" from my trusty backpack that I had been studying earlier in the day. I find and read out the spell of "Coming Forth by Day."

"Come my soul, O you wardens of the sky, if you delay letting my soul see my corpse, you will find the eye of Horus standing up thus against you . . . The great god, Osiris, and his son, Horus, will proceed in peace when you allow this soul to find his body. He is vindicated by the gods . . . May his soul see this body, may it return to this body, which will never be destroyed or perish," I read.

Queen Setibhor lifts her head and raises her eyes in blessing and then leaving her hand on the Eye of Horus and the other on the Sacred Scarab, "REBIRTH!" she demands. The light emanating from her is blinding. She smiles a smile that transcends time.

"I foretold we would meet again," she says, handing the scarab back to me. The WAS sceptre magically appears in her hand. "This is yours." The pink cloud and Setibhor vanish. I am holding the WAS sceptre.

The blood on Nathan's face and head dries and falls away. Kneeling, I cradle his head is my lap. He opens his eyes.

"Hey, Jono, what happened?"

"Well, the tomb fell on you," I laugh. "You had the help of Her Majesty, the Great Royal Wife Setibhor, and your Horus amulet. I don't know what will happen if you return to the present though. Anyway, you were a goner."

I rub the Scarab until it glows. Khepri stands, his arms stretched over us. Nathan and I each have a hand on the scarab. The space becomes dark! Lights flash! Swoosh! The scarab whirls us back to the present.

I crawl into the open and wave to the paramedics. They lift the weak but alive Nathan out of the tomb and into the sunshine. Once they put him inside, they shut the ambulance door. I see Khepri-Ra standing at the gaping hole into the tomb.

Nathan has survived. I must repeat it to myself to believe it. Nathan was dead. He is back. The WAS sceptre is in my possession, but invisible. I can feel it. Egypt has its magic. Egypt has its secrets.

Dad comes to my side. "I don't know what you two did, but it worked. I would really like it if you would tell me sometime."

Zahra comes, takes my hand, and walks with me as I cry and then laugh. My best friend is back.

***

Early the next morning, I'm off to the Luxor hospital.

"Nathan," I say, entering his room, "you're looking better than last night!"

"You always flatter me," he says, smiling.

"I want you to know it's more than that. I really care for you. I love you."

We look into each other's eyes. We know it is true.

Later, Dad comes into the hospital to see Nathan. "Well, Nathan, you look pretty good for someone who has been to hell and back." We laugh. It is so good to see Nathan alive and laughing with us.

"It surprised the doctor. I just have some of bruising. He's seen nothing like it. I think I might leave with you today!"

"What?" I say, but of course I believe it. It was only a precaution that he came to the hospital.

I'm looking at Nathan and smiling when he says, "All right, Jonathan. Stop looking at me. I'm here. I'm alive."

I realize I have changed. You can't experience what I have and not be different.

CHAPTER TWELVE
KHENTKAUS' SECRET

The next morning, Zahra gets time off work to be here when Nathan comes back to the dig. "Listen, Nathan, are you sure you're really up to this?" she asks.

"Never better. Can't wait," he replies.

"Okay," I say, "but if you need a break, take one. I've been thinking . . ." He gives me a look. Right, I know. He is suggesting I never stop. Too right. "When we were working on Khentkaus' tomb, there were pictures in the chapel area of the queen and her architect. Now this is not unusual, but he appears several times and is always standing close to her. He also isn't a member of the royal family so should be painted as much smaller. I couldn't find any information on him, but he was important to her."

Zahra offers her idea on the tomb. "I know it sounds improbable, but I think there's a secret here. Since we exposed a lower level with the help of the earthquake, no one has properly examined the floor. So, let's do it." Her eyes sparkle with the excitement of a new challenge. We all head down to the bottom level where the team has cleared away any sand and rubble. We get our brushes going on the floor of the chamber, believing there is something more to Khentkaus' tomb.

After several hours of being hunched over or working on our knees, Nathan yells, "Over here!"

He has discovered glyphs carved into the flooring reading, "Khentkaus Lives," followed by her cartouche. We brush around the blocks and then use tools to scrape out the mortar between them. Finally, we pry a block out, then another, until we have excavated an opening. Brushing more, we remove sand and dust so we can see a sizable 18 centimetre metal box. We work hard to free it and lift it. It finally moves. I look around the top edge for a clue to open it. Then I see a small hole and insert the awl of my Swiss army knife. The lid opens slightly, then I apply a slight bit of pressure.

In the box is a gold container with the lid fashioned as the head of a young man. He has a youthful look about him, a secretive smile. There is a seal on the lid. The gold container has hieroglyphs arranged in a pattern interspersed with gemstones. Zahra reads the inscription. "I have buried my heart in your tomb, my love, so that it will be with you in eternity, Loving Companion."

I ramble, "Has he buried his heart in her tomb? This is against the belief of the ancients. The heart is left in the mummy as it is the home of the 'Ka.' I don't think this container is big enough to hold a heart. Probably frankincense or myrrh, I think I can smell something."

"I think the box is silver," Nathan whispers.

"Silver was more precious than gold because it had to be imported," adds Zahra.

"Where is his heart?" I ask.

We remove a few more flooring slabs and dig deeper into the ground under the tomb. We find a box shaped like a small sarcophagus. His name is never given, but the lid of the box has the same words as the silver box: 'I have buried my heart in your tomb, my love, so that it will be with you in eternity, Loving Companion.' The miniature sarcophagus is beautifully inlaid with Isis, goddess of love on the four sides, her wings spread so she encloses it. On the lid is Nekbet protector of Egypt, her huge wings spread across the whole area.

"I don't think we should open this box," Zahra says. "We can guess what is in it."

"I think I should get Dr. Czerny to come look at the silver box. The miniature sarcophagus should stay here," I say.

Everyone agrees. I place the sarcophagus back in the hole. Nathan gently places handfuls of dirt on top and we replace all but one of the floor slabs.

Nathan gets the doctor gets out of bed, but he's not thrilled. "You know you shouldn't be working on your own."

"We only had a hunch," Nathan explains. "They painted Khentkaus with her architect several times. He's the wrong size, too tall for a commoner. It seems strange."

We get out of Dr. Czerny's way. There isn't much room in the burial chamber.

"We started by brushing the floor, and then, on a few of the flooring blocks, we saw her cartouche. This was underneath," I explain.

"I am not sure how to read these glyphs," Zahra says, asking for the Doctor's help. It might just be a way to get him involved.

"'Loving Companion' is inscribed on the gold vessel," the Egyptologist says. "I'll take these to the examination tent where there's more light. Tomorrow we can explore more of the floor. This is very unusual. Very unusual," Dr. Czerny says as he leaves with the silver box.

"I guess Khentkaus had a close relationship after all," I say.

The scarab in my jeans pocket starts moving, but I ignore it. We wander over to the examination tent where there are always drinks. On the tables are statues, some restored and some complete. There is Khnum, the ram-headed god, Atum the Creator, a broken one of Horus, a gold statue of Set, jewellery, bracelets, gold chains, and a group of gods and goddesses made of gold, silver, and electrum. The family of statues. The silver box and gold vase from the floor are also there.

"What I remember when I look at this wonderful display of treasures is how hard they were to dig out. The ground, soil, whatever you want to call it, was hard. It had solidified under the weight of the tomb and the centuries. Trowel, trowel, brush, brush, in order to get each object," Zahra recalls.

"I want a cup of coffee. Anyone else?" I ask.

"Not me. Maybe tea," Zahra replies.

We sit around a table in the tent.

"How did we know to check the floor? Seems really weird," I ask.

"I thought there was something else to that little room. That led me to check the floor," Zahra offers.

"Yeah, all that decoration," I say "She was almost always painted alone unless she was painted with her architect. Where was her husband, Neferirkare? A very simple explanation is the king would have to be painted twice the size of Khentkaus and they didn't have the room. But there was nothing in the burial chamber but the sarcophagus and the jars. Seemed like there was a secret to Khentkaus II."

"Right. Of course," Nathan replies.

Late that night, Dad comes to my tent. "I'm sorry, I have no right to ask you this, but I have to." I wonder what's going on. "I don't know if you've been able to have any kind of chat with your mother recently, but my sense, mostly from Peggy, is that she is not very well. Much worse than when we left. I think it would be helpful if you were there." I can see his concern. His usual jaunty attitude is gone. "I would go if I could, but I have a contract for two more months."

I'm not keen to go home as I'm building a life here. "I'll check with both Mum and Auntie Peggy," I tell him.

"Thanks so much, son."

I check on the time. It's noon in Vancouver. I can phone home. Aunt Peggy answers.

"Hi there," I say.

Before I can say any more, Aunt Peggy dumps out her concerns. "Oh, Jonathan, I'm so glad you phoned. I'd get her to the phone, but she's sleeping. She doesn't always sleep well at night. The fact is, Jonathan, your mother is not doing well. There have been frequent ups and downs, but lately she's just going down." I can tell she's disturbed by Mum's condition. "I really think it would help if you came home."

"I'll let you know my flight times. Give my love to Mum," I reply. I guess I'm going home.

I walk out of my tent and along the ridge above the tomb of Khentkaus. Her tomb is cursed, I'm sure of it. Then I find Dad in his tent. "I made a commitment to Aunt Peggy that I'd go home." He nods solemnly. "You asked me to tell you what happened to Nathan when the tomb collapsed," I continue. "I need to tell you the truth. As you know, the floor slipped, and Zahra fell. Then we pulled it apart and invaded Khentkaus' burial chamber. Why didn't we realize the danger? I don't know. There were engineers on the team. Anyway, then there was an earthquake. I jumped into the hole, not thinking about my fear of enclosed spaces. Nathan was dead, but I took him back in time. Nathan was saved by Heka, the divine magic and power possessed by the Great Wife, Lady of the Two Lands, Setibhor. You remember she stepped out of the painting in Keknebithor's tomb. I read from *The Book of Coming Forth by Day* as she held the pectoral of Horus and the Sacred Scarab. Then it happened. He came back to life."

I look at him. I've told him something he doesn't want to believe. Trips to the past are one thing but bringing Nathan back from the dead is something else.

He looks at me with new respect. I have a connection with ancient Egypt that he doesn't have. We both have a new awareness of the power of the ancient Gods and Kings.

***

The next morning, I head over to the admin tent to find Dr. Czerny. He is very understanding when I tell him my situation.

"Family, family, family should always come first. I often forget that, but I'm always grateful when I'm reminded and have a chance to go home."

After chatting with both Dad and Dr. Czerny, I arrange for a flight back to Vancouver.

Nathan and Abdoullah both insist on taking me to the airport. I want to just slip away, but no. Abdoullah gives me flowers, some Egyptian custom I don't think anyone has ever heard of. My hand is shaken over and over by the entire crew, and if that isn't enough, I'm hugged several times.

At the airport, Nathan and Abdoullah hug me yet again. "I'm coming back, you know," I say emphatically.

"Yes, but when? I'll miss you," Nathan says with another hug, and then Abdoullah says the same and gives me another hug. Thank god they call my flight. Secretly I may not like all the fuss but, I'm grateful to have such great friends.

CHAPTER THIRTEEN

TO VANCOUVER FOR MUM

A few days later, I'm driving down our street and notice that everything is the same. So weird. I pay the taxi driver and walk up the drive. Rex comes running out and jumps up. Mum stands in the doorway smiling.

"I'm so glad to have my boy home! You've filled out and have a good tan."

"Well, you're looking pretty good yourself." The truth is, she's lost weight. Not looking too healthy. "I think I'd better run around with Rex for a few minutes so he'll give us some peace," I say as Rex continues to jump up. Rex and I run around the block and a few minutes later, head inside. Rex is able to sit, but his tail keeps wagging.

There are hugs all around. Peggy is glad to have some support. I can tell by how long and hard she hugs me.

"You really do need looking after," Mum says.

"You do. You're looking thin," Aunt Peggy joins in.

So, over the next few days, I have some great meals and wonderful desserts. There's lots of strawberry shortcake.

"Well, strawberries are in season," Aunt Peggy explains. Of course, there are all kinds of cookies: peanut butter, chocolate chip, and aggression cookies with chocolate chips and walnuts. Aunt Peggy is known for her squares, so there are lots of those too, mainly nut smacks and Nanaimo bars. She says she knew Happy Hall, who invented them. Then she brings out matrimonial cake. Is that a hint? I think the underlying message is, "A guy should come home more."

I spend all my time with Mum and Rex, of course, walking through the park and our neighbourhood. We have always told Egyptian stories as we walk. Mum recalls her telling me the story of Horus and Set.

"Do you remember the famous stone boat race?" I ask.

"Of course, but you tell it to me this time," Mum says.

I begin. "The race was between Set and Horus. They made a bet for the throne of Egypt. They would have a boat race in stone boats. Horus was clever, and his boat was made of wood painted to resemble stones rather than truly made of stone. Set's boat, being made of stone, sank. Horus, the smart guy, won the race, and Set lost the throne. Horus took the fertile lands in the Nile Valley. Set took the desert. The Egyptians have been celebrating humour for six thousand years. Pretty tricky."

Mum and I share a love of nature of the outdoors. We go to Stanley Park and wander through the forest trails lined with giant Douglas Fir trees and Lost Lagoon filled with water lilies, ducks, and a shooting fountain. I push Mum's wheelchair all around the perimeter of the park and experience the calming effect of the waves slapping on the shore of the Sea Wall.

On another day, we visit Sun Yet Sen Garden, an authentic Chinese garden in the centre of the city with incredible serenity. Lovely Chinese tea houses and authenic buildings surround the reflection pools, moss covered rocks, and weeping trees. As we walk along a wooden section of the path, we see the mirroring central lake start reflecting dark clouds. It looks like rain. The brightly coloured koi swim serenely, unaware of the brewing storm. Mum and I take shelter on the porch of one of the larger bamboo-flanked buildings. Silently, Set appears in His storm cloud.

"I have you to myself, Jonathan," Set says. "What a nice, scenic place you have found. I imagine your scarab is at home and your WAS sceptre is forgotten. I call upon the gods of evil to support me."

Mum and I see the colourful evil but exotic gods of Set's cohort appear between the trees and shrubs of the garden. All at once, Set's confidence is shattered by Ra's brilliant beams piercing Set's dark cloud.

Khepri appears floating in the air. "How like you, Set, to disturb the tranquility of this peaceful place. This woman needs solace; needs time with her son. Your insensitivity does not belong here." The strong light of Ra pierces Set's cloud and silences Set and his companions. They slink into the sky. Khepri's soothing purple mist surrounds Mother and me and we relax in it.

***

It's only a few days later that I'm silently sitting by her bed, listening to her breathe. I can't stand her getting weaker. I take my scarab out and rub it. Nothing happens. I rub it again. The familiar purple mist surrounds me. Khepri stands facing me.

"I know why you have called me. You have a request. Restore your mother to health."

"Please. I love her."

"There is a time: a time to live, a time to die. Your mother's body has outlived its time. She enjoyed life in all its stages, growing, learning, loving. Now she is ready for resting, for the Field of Reeds. She is ready to be relieved of illness. The power of the gods cannot counter the course of life. You have enjoyed her time with you. You can enjoy the memories of her time with you. She had great pride in giving you life and seeing you grow into a man. Now give back; give her rest."

Khepri disappears in his purple mist, taking with him my selfishness.

Then Dad comes home. We both sit by her bed, but she chats less and less.

Soon, we're sitting by her coffin, Dad, Aunt Peggy, and I.

The ancient Egyptians didn't believe death was the end. They built tombs and filled them with everything the deceased would need. I have a garland of carnations made, her favourite flower, and put it around her neck and continue it around on her chest, like on the mummies I have seen.

I'm numb. I feel loss, but Dad and I have things to look after. I need to be strong for Peggy. She has lost a lifelong friend: her sister. I help Dad organize the funeral service, notify Mom's law firm, put an obituary in the paper, and contact cousins.

Dad is really grieving. He finds me and Rex at the beach and sits beside me. We both speak of Mum's caring, her patience, her acceptance. We are very aware of how proud she was of her law firm. Dad wants me to know she was also very proud of me. I don't think I deserve it, but he said she certainly was. I will really miss her warmth, her willingness to take time for me, to listen, to understand. I appreciate what a significant person she was to me.

Finally, I cry. I cry because I have lost the most caring person in my life. I have survived the weirdest experience in that tomb in Egypt.

Nathan died and came back. But my mother just wasted away from this horrible disease. I wish I could have helped her.

"How are you doing, Dad?" I ask, my tears briefly halting.

"I could have been a better husband. I didn't cheat or anything like that, but I didn't spend enough time with Beth. Work kept me going to Egypt."

"I think we have something in common: guilt. We should have acknowledged how important she really was to us."

The celebration of Mum's life is simple. To me, it's a blur really. There are so many people here, in her church, friends from many years of her life, organizations she belonged to, friends she had helped, the church she had supported.

The remembrance service is simple. Her minister says, "Elizabeth, Beth, wife, mother, has been important to so many as we can see evidenced here today."

We sing "The Garden," which starts with the line, "I come to the garden alone when the dew is still on the roses." I remember Mum's love of gardening and her pride in her beautiful roses.

Some people who Mum worked with spoke, thanking her for her legal aid and the time she donated to the community.

Aunt Peggy reads a poem she loves that makes her think of Mum.

> "She is Gone"
>
> You can shed tears that she is gone
>
> Or you can smile because she has lived.
>
> You can close your eyes and pray that she will come back
>
> Or you can open your eyes and see all that she has left.
>
> Your heart can be empty because you can't see her

Or you can be full of the love that you shared.

You can turn your back on tomorrow and live yesterday

Or you can be happy for tomorrow because of yesterday.

You can remember her and only that she is gone

Or you can cherish her memory and let it live on.

You can cry and close your mind, be empty and turn your back

Or you can do what she would want: smile, open your eyes, love, and go on."[1]

We sing "Morning has Broken" because I remember Mum reading Eleanor Farjeon's poems and stories to me. Most people think of Cat Stevens, but I remember that English writer Farjeon wrote the words. There are refreshments in the church hall organized by Mum's friends at the church.

As we file out of the cemetery, I see a shadow move behind a granite mausoleum. "Dad, keep an eye open. There's someone sneaking around. Over behind me."

---

[1]This poem by David Harkins has been given to public domain and was used at Queen Mother Elizabeth's funeral.

As we drive home, Dad says, “Are you sure you saw someone sneaking around?”

“As sure as we’re sitting here.”

After that, Dad keeps looking in the rear-view mirror. “Ah ha!” he breathes. “There is a car following us. Until we turned into Point Grey, I wasn’t sure.”

“What should we do?”

“Do you still have a gun at home?” I ask.

“Yeah, in my bedside table,” Dad answers.

“I think a call to the RCMP or the Vancouver police might be in order.”

“The RCMP might be more interested in an international case,” Dad responds.

When we get home, Dad picks up the landline and chats with a member.

“Yes, This is Dr. Darryl Johnsten. I’m an Egyptologist and my son and I have a few valuable items in our home from Egypt. We had some trouble in Egypt recently, and we just had a car follow us across town. Is there any way you could have a car drive by our home in Point Grey? We live close to the university endowment lands.”

He gives our address and the officer says they'll check our complaint.

I'm nervous. My mother has just died and now some creep is following us. I'm feeling kind of, well, not at my best. Vulnerable. I left Gorman in the past, so how could some guy know to tail us?

We have a reasonable night, then just before daybreak, I'm awakened by a crash. I throw on a bathrobe and run towards my dad's room, but he's already in the hall, gun in hand.

"Where did that crash come from?" I ask.

"Downstairs. My office I think."

As we go, I phone the RCMP, telling them about the noise.

"Wait for us," The operator replies.

We proceed to the office anyway. The door is partially open, and we can see two guys going through Dad's stuff.

"Okay, what are you guys doing here?" Dad boldly asks.

The shocked look on their faces is so comical. "The professor's son asked us to, ah, to find a big beetle."

"Well, I suggest you find a seat here and we discuss this calmly. My son owns the beetle in question—actually it's a scarab—and he's not prepared to give it to you. Now, where did you meet the professor?"

"We, ah, we, ah, met him . . ."

"No, we worked for him," the other guy corrects.

"Yeah, about six months ago. We went to Egypt, then he just disappeared," the first thug says. "We met up with his son, Rick."

"Funny thing that. We were on a trip and decided Gorman wasn't much fun to be with, so we left him behind," I explain.

Dad's really enjoying this, but RCMP members soon rush into the office. He recovers quickly.

"Officers, these two gentlemen were attempting robbery. They smashed the glass in the front door to gain entry. Can you take them into custody?"

"We would love to. Please put your hands behind your backs," one officer says.

"Tell us, Dr. Johnsten," says another officer, "why are these men being so cooperative?"

Before Dad or I can answer, one of the robbers says, "He's got magic. He made our boss disappear."

"Vivid imagination," I retort quickly.

"Well, it worked. Thank you." They take the bad guys away.

I run upstairs and throw on some clothes. When I return I find Dad checking Mum's plants.

I smile watching him and I ask, "Coffee, Dad?"

Aunt Peggy comes into the kitchen in her pink chenille bathrobe. "Were those police officers I saw leaving?" she wonders aloud.

"Yes," Dad replies. "Glad you slept through it."

"Coffee? I'm just putting some on," I ask Aunt Peggy.

"That would be very nice. I'll make some toast," Aunt Peggy offers.

"How do you like your eggs, Margaret?" Dad asks.

"Boiled. Three and a half minutes please, Darryl."

"Jonathan?"

"Two eggs, over easy," I answer.

"So, what did I miss? I thought you two were evading the question right from the time I came down."

"Well, Aunt Peggy, Dad and I were both awakened by a crash. We came downstairs to find two thugs in Dad's office."

"I never!" Aunt Peggy exclaims. "What did they hope to get? Your wallet, car keys? There seems to be more and more crime in the city. Not like it used to be."

"I think you're right on both counts, robbery and more crime," I answered.

"Eggs are ready!" Dad calls.

"Speaking of ready, what are you two planning on doing next?" Peggy asks.

"You mean besides eating eggs and toast?" I laugh.

"You have a girl in Egypt. Your mother told me. Kept me up to date. And Nathan is still there?" Aunt Peggy sure likes to pry. No, I think she cares.

"Yes, he's there and we have plans." I really don't want to talk about Zahra with her.

"Well, I need to get home," Peggy confesses. "My cat, not to mention all my plants, were supposedly left in the care of a friend, but it's not really the same, is it? Oh, Jonathan, your mother asked me to give you this. Open it when you're alone. Now I'll be wondering what plans you men are hatching," Peggy continues.

"That's a quaint way of saying it," I reply. "Especially after having eggs for breakfast."

"Now listen, Jonathan, I expect a letter telling me what you are doing. I have a computer now, so you can send one of those emails."

Dad explains, "Well, I have all my notes from the four tombs I excavated this past season to write up. Then, I must think of returning to the university for the next two semesters. Jonathan, you?"

"I've been thinking about going to the American University in Cairo. Nathan and I are both talking of going there. We can take all their courses and finally get a degree to work with you, Dad."

"I'm glad you have something in mind, but it will take you four years or more to complete your studies. Don't include me in your plans. Life has devious ways of changing things. I may have retired by then, or I might be doing some museum work."

I guess he's right, but I feel like he's pushing me away. Maybe he's just being realistic. I'm independent, so I should be able to think before I feel.

A week later, I help Dad with the probate of Mum's will. She left me some money and some of her mother's jewellery. Dad, of course, gets the bulk of the estate. Anyway, things are all tied up.

I hear from the American University in Cairo, and I'm officially accepted. I think it was a formality as they had already accepted me for field work. Nathan says he has been accepted too.

***

Aunt Peggy soon returns home and Dad starts going in to the university to complete his paperwork.

I spend my days walking along the beach in front of our property with Rex. Today I sit on one of the big logs and hold the envelope that Aunt Peggy gave me. What does Mum want me to know? I open the envelope and try to read the letter. I can't. It's hard to read with tears in your eyes. I can't get past, *"Dear Jonathan, my son."* I put it back in the envelope and stuff it into my shirt pocket. I will read it one day, when I can really focus on it. Right now, Rex wants to play fetch.

As I walk along the beach with Rex, I'm aware these logs have been here for years; they have a silver-grey sheen to them. As beautiful as home is, Zahra, Nathan, and Egypt are calling me. Dad begins taking Rex for walks so he can adjust to my absence again. I book a flight for the following week.

I'm super excited to be going back to Egypt. I have a novel to read on the flight and there are movies I can watch, and frequent meals. I also have Dad's book *Curses and Spells from Ancient Egypt*. I find it strangely comforting, reading about the dead who never die but who journey to the next life. I find a series of chapters on communicating with the dead, but soon fall asleep.

Suddenly, a voice is saying, "Sir, sir!" and a woman is shaking me. I look at her with dazed eyes.

"Sorry," she says. "You were moaning. I thought it couldn't be a pleasant dream."

"Thank you. No, it wasn't." Nathan was screaming all over again. The past is with me, in my dreams.

CHAPTER FOURTEEN

BACK IN EGYPT

The hot, thick air of Egypt hits me the moment I'm thrust out of the airport terminal. *They say it hits you like a wall. It's true, I tell ya.* That's what I thought when Nathan and I came to Egypt just six months ago.

I contacted a couple of people before I came, and here they are, Nathan and Abdoullah! The big man comes up to me and gives me an enormous hug. Nathan just smiles.

"Yo, Jono. Great to see you, man," Nathan says.

"You too."

"Sorry to hear about your mother."

"Thanks. It's been rough."

"Ah, Mister Jonathan, so good to see you here in the land of your heart," Abdoullah interjects.

"It's good to see you as well, As-salaam Alykum."

Abdoullah laughs. It's so good to hear his laugh. "Very well done. Almost as good as a real Egyptian."

"Oh, shit," Nathan says, "Come here!" He gives me a very sincere hug. We're so happy to be alive and together again.

We head to the site and arrive in time for the morning coffee break. Zahra arrives shortly after and we're so glad to be back together. We give each other hugs and kisses. Then we get in a huddle with Nathan and Abdoullah. I tell my trio, "I've been thinking."

"Here we go again," Nathan laughs.

"When I found the scarab almost ten years ago, a papyrus manuscript covered it. I've transcribed it and it contains a message of a tomb and what we can find there. I think it would be worth a look before school starts in the Fall. It might be a wild goose chase. Before you ask, Abdoullah, there is no wild goose and we are not chasing anything, except our dreams."

"Those crazy English sayings," Abdullah mumbles.

"Count me in," Zahra, Nathan, and Abdoullah quickly respond to the adventure I described. We go into the mess tent and get a cup of coffee. Of course, Zahra has tea. We sit around a table.

Nathan is daydreaming of finding a tomb with some special objects—alabaster, silver, gold, lapis, maybe a trip to the past to meet the owner—when Zahra speaks and gets everyone's attention. Reality. She knows about the government regulations. "Several things need to be considered: I have a job. This will not be a vacation. It's going to be very hot work. And we may not get a permit. The Department of Antiquities is currently trying to find several missing tombs themselves. So, we may not be welcome. It might be best if we're looking for a tomb not found on the Department of Antiquities' list."

"Lots to consider," I realize. "Well, what we know is that the papyrus says, 'amen neb bw m sstaa mehit en nsw bity hm,' followed by the ideogram of the king and his name, 'ah mes.' That translates as 'You must hide all of the treasure in the secret tomb of His Majesty the King, Nebpehtyre Ahmose.'"

"His name means, 'The Lord of Strength is Re, the Moon is Born.' The moon god is the defender," Zahra adds.

"I did more research," I continue. "There is a pyramid belonging to Ahmose at Abousir. What's weird is that they buried the other kings of the same dynasty in the Valley of the Kings. Although the pyramid interior has not been explored since 1902, work in 2006 uncovered portions of a massive mud-brick construction ramp built against its face."

"Other Egyptologists supposedly found his mummy in 1881," Zahra states. "It was placed with fifty mummies disturbed by robbers, and they were in a tomb in the Valley of the Kings named "the Royal cache." So, the question is, is his tomb at Abousir in his pyramid or in the Valley of the Kings? We don't know where to look. Another thing to consider is if the identification of all these royal mummies is valid."

"When you spoke, you looked anxious," I say.

"It's a big decision," she responds.

"Nathan, what are you thinking?"

"If there is a possibility of finding his mummy in the valley, and since the papyrus says tomb, not pyramid, then I think we should try the valley."

"Abdoullah, you've shown the valley to many tourists. What do you think?" I ask.

"There are so many, many tombs there. King Tutankhamen's tomb was buried under rubble they dumped from the other tombs. We need a clue where to look in the right place!" the big man says. I place the papyrus on the table.

Checking the papyrus I say, "Here, Zahra, please read this again. I may have missed something."

"Down here, where it's torn. Do you have the pieces?" she asks.

"Yeah, but they're difficult to read," I reply. I take out an envelope in my backpack and hand to her. Zahra opens her purse and takes out a pair of flat tweezers and removes the fragile pieces from the envelope and places them carefully on the table.

"Look, if we fit these three pieces together in the bottom corner, we can see they make a sentence. It reads: 'Not too close, but not too far, just up the way of kings," Zahra continues. "Wow, that really helps."

"This is what we know," I begin. "The family of Seqenenre Tao fought the Hyksos invaders, and he was killed in the war, as was his son, Kamose. Ahmose finally achieved victory, backed by his mother Ahhotep I, known as the warrior queen. They finally drove the Hyksos invaders from Egypt. Ahhotep I was buried in the tomb of her son's wife Ahhotep II. The tomb of Ahhotep II contained her now destroyed mummy and jewellery of gold and silver. There were also daggers and an inscribed ceremonial axe blade made of copper and electrum and wood. There were also the three golden flies. Now the golden flies seem strange to us, but they were the highest order that could be given to anyone. They were three beautifully fashioned large flies with delicate wings on a gold chain.

The golden flies seem strange to us, but they were like the Victoria Cross to the Egyptians: the honour that was given to anyone usually a commander, but not always," I state. I pause and think.

"So, the question is," Nathan wonders aloud, "would they have buried Ahmose near his brother, father, and mother, or was he thinking of new beginnings?

If he were buried closer to his family, they could have buried him in the Valley of the Kings, close to his father, mother, and brother. Another possibility is he was buried near the valley, but not right in it."

I point out, "I noticed that most tombs are close together or even crossing above or below other tombs. But there is a space between KV1 and KV 2."

"Okay, okay," Nathan interrupts, "What are these crazy numbers?"

"Sorry, bro," I say, once you know it will seem easy. The KV stands for Kings Valley, backwards I know and then each tomb in the valley is numbered. I should have made sure everyone was on the same page."

"Or at least in the book," Nathan laughs.

Zahra says. "I think we need the name of a noted Egyptologist, preferably an Egyptian one, to get us a permit. More local Egyptologists are being given permits."

I contact the former Director of the Egyptian Department of Antiquities, Dr. Hawass. He recommends a couple of Egyptologists, including Dr, Wright. After Dr. Czerny interviews several people, Dr. Wright and an Egyptian right out of university, Dr. Khaled, he hires them to take on the project.

"Name dropper," Zahra says. "Dr. Hawass is the Director of the Egyptian Antiquities. Famous because he travels the world and speaks."

We set up a camp just outside the valley, out of the way of tour buses. The best time to work is early in the morning late in the evening. We just need to wait for Dr. Wright and Dr. Khaled.

Oddly enough, Dr. Wright was the man we met at the Vancouver Airport when Nathan and I were first coming over. He's a very friendly guy with a no-nonsense approach. He and I both like to run, so in the cool of the early morning, we run for a kilometre just as the sun is rising. When the papers come, we start work.

The doctors read the papyrus and the bottom of the scarab but give no comment. We talk about our experience and they talk of theirs. Then Dr. Khaled says, "You found this scarab and papyrus in Saqqara?"

"Yes, when I was ten, my first dig."

"Any chance they're fake?"

"I dug them up myself. Imbedded in the hard soil or clay of the tomb. They were in a box that had disintegrated but had gold straps."

"Sorry I doubted. I always check but with that provenance, they could not be fake." Dr. Wright smiles his agreement.

***

This dig is different than the others I've been on, because of my memories. Early in the morning, we start excavating. The huge pile of rubble is loose because the area has been searched before. I'm not expecting anything to come of our efforts. I wish I were more positive, but it's almost like waiting for the other shoe to fall. What is really bothering me?

The second day, the government inspector comes out to see us. He is a friend of Dr. Khaled, and they chat away. "I'm not hopeful. The area has been excavated before." Tell us something we don't know. "Watch the cliff," the inspector warns before leaving.

We all look up as the sun blazes down. The cliff above the tomb entrance does seem to be unstable or maybe not. We retreat until late afternoon each day before starting our second shift.

Zahra and I take a few tours of the nearby tombs. Ramesses VI's tomb is next to us, famous for its great paintings.

The painters of the repeated pictures of the king and Osiris have given them unique personal features. We like the coolness of the tomb and its fans. The large square columns that are a famous part of that tomb are brightly painted. The burial chamber has a vaulted ceiling with mirror images of Nut, Goddess of the Sky, and passages from *The Book of the Day* and *The Book of the Night.*

Mostly, we really enjoyed the time alone together.

Finally, we get back to work and start making progress. A tunnel is opening up, but better still, the floor and walls are carved into the rock. "Was this just a former excavation, or is it a passage into a tomb?"

"I'm not positive," Dr. Wright says, "but if the tunnel slopes down, we may be onto something."

Nathan is wandering around outside the tunnel when he calls in to Dr. Wright. "Won't your dog get hot in the car?"

"Don't have a dog," Dr. Wright answers. Nathan and I exchange a glance and I go out to look. Right, no dog. I look around. I think if anyone could see Set, I can.

A week goes by. We all watch the cliff and I watch for Set. We dig and use barrows to move the rock we excavate. Then we hit the wall. If we're to make progress, we need help.

Early the next morning, the first group of helpers arrives and assesses the job. We hammer wedges between the blocks.

"All right, Abdoullah, do your magic." I hand him the ANKH. It takes several minutes, but soon the block next to the inserted ANKH begins to slowly move forward.

Doctors Wright, Khaled and Czerny watch with amazement. "The good thing about this sealed wall is it suggests the site hasn't been robbed," Dr. Wright says.

Nathan, Abdoullah, and I put our muscles to work with the government team. We pry the blocks out, some falling to the floor where they are slid along with the aid of water right out of the tomb. We rig lights and run cables and more lights.

Then there it is; Ahmose I's tomb. I'm disappointed at what I see, then I realize I can't distinguish the objects stacked inside.

Zahra hugs me. Nathan and Abdoullah are "oooing" and "ahhing." Slowly, we take a box from the top layer of contents. Zahra hurries out to phone the Luxor Museum to get workers to come so we can keep the artefacts secure.

We dust the first box carefully with brushes. The top of the chest has a fantastic portrait of the king, his overbite and hooked nose, standing left foot forward, mace held high, captured for eternity. On the sides of the box are inlaid figures of Isis and Nephthys giving balanced magic. The box contains the four canopic jars in separate compartments with the heads of the sons of Horus: Imsety, Duamutef, Hapi, and Qebehsenuef. When I see them, they amaze me, the fine detail of the carved, painted alabaster.

There are boxes packed with statues, lamps, and bottles of ointments that still have a pleasant scent after thousands of years. The ancient priests stacked makeup, mirrors, furniture, couches, beds, and chariots carefully in the tomb. The king's weapons, swords, and long knives are laid out to prepare him for the afterlife. Beautifully embossed gold fans, whose feathers disintegrate and fall to the floor when we touch them, lie in an arranged group.

As we welcome the museum curators to catalogue this treasure, the cliff slides with a horrific sound. We're all frozen for a second. Once the dust settles, several of us run towards the entrance. We see a pile of rubble completely blocking the entrance.

We go back into the main room of the tomb, sit on the floor, and regroup.

Dr. Wright asks, "Do we have some shovels on this side of the landslide?"

"Well, there's one," Abdoullah responds.

I'm reading through a book of Dad's that I had in my trusty backpack.

"Here we are trapped in a tomb, and you're sitting there reading," Nathan jokes.

"It's a section of *The Coming Forth by Day*. It worked on you, and I thought maybe we could get some ancient workers to help."

"You mean resurrect them?" Dr. Khaled says in a stunned voice. "Really, Jonathan, that sounds insane."

"Well, anything is possible," I say flippantly.

I stand and look towards the boxes and exposed figures from the tomb, then read aloud, "O you guards, you are called to come forth to keep the gates because of Osiris. O you who guard them and who report the affairs of the Two Lands to Osiris every day, I know you and I know your names. We call all who serve the king. Guard him and protect him. You gods and goddesses arise, you servants arise. The time has come. Osiris has need of you; Isis has need of you; Set has need of you; Anubis has need of you."

There's a whirring sound and soon the golden cloud of the supernatural surrounds us. There is movement. As the mist thickens, the sound in the tomb becomes louder. We see Isis, Nephthys, the guardians of the king's sarcophagus come forward, their gold leaf shimmering, their eyes outlined, beautified with kohl. They move gracefully. Anubis, the crouching black jackal, God of the Dead, weigher of souls, stretches his long legs, raises his head, and howls. He is accompanied in his resurrection by Set.

The gods and goddesses move forward. Nephthys, the mother of Anubis, strokes Anubis' sleek head and back. Happy to be alive, Anubis howls again.

The four divinities lead a small army of guards toward us. Then a contingent of shabtis appear, 365, one for each day of the year, now growing from doll-like statuettes into human-sized servants, ready to do their master's bidding.

"What the hell is going on?" Nathan demands.

The army of the awakened grabs us and pushes us or throws us back into the tomb. Some of us are thrown with sufficient force to make us fall on the floor or against tomb furniture.

The army continues marching toward the slide, rapidly moving the stones and earth as if by magic.

"It's working!" I shout. Then I realize they will soon be escaping into the outside world. I realize I have unleashed an army from the afterlife.

I yell, "Isis, Goddess of Love, help us!" She turns, smiles her beautiful smile, but continues the march.

Then there is an amazing flash of light as Osiris, reborn as King Ahmose, his hands gripping a crook and flail, steps forward, pushes through the tomb furniture, and strides forward. The four-metre-high king is impressive, scary, breathtaking.

Zahra yells, "Jonathan, do something!"

I pull out my scarab and rub it frantically. I look back. King Ahmose is marching forward.

I keep rubbing desperately. The familiar purple cloud coalesces around me. Finally, Khepri appears.

He has never shouted at me before, but now he does. "What have you done? You have awakened the Gods and Goddesses of the Afterlife!"

"Please help me, Lord Khepri-Ra!"

With my most fervent plea, Ra, greatest of all the gods, appears. His light brightens until it blinds. The Gods stop, the guards stop, the Ushabtis stop, but Osiris-Ahmose does not stop. Out of the mist, Maat and Thoth move towards us, screaming strange oaths in horror at this revolution of the cosmic order. The gods and goddesses turn around, facing the inside of the tomb. The light of Ra focuses on the gigantic face of Osiris-Ahmose. Blinded, Osiris-Ahmose stops. With a resounding crack, the great king shudders, converts to granite, cracks, shatters and crashes with enormous impact at our feet.

"Bow, mortals! Bow!" Ra shouts, shaking the tomb. We grovel. The gods and goddesses acknowledge our supplication, complete their turn, and retreat. The goddesses stand guard once more at the corners of Ahmose's sarcophagus. The guards restack themselves in the huge cupboards. Anubis once more stands at the entrance of the tomb. The shabti begin shrinking as they lie down on the examination tables or on the floor.

We humans exhale an enormous sigh. At that moment, the crew, who have been working to free us from the outside, burst through the remaining debris.

The first crewman through says, "You sure did a lot of work to remove this much earth and rocks."

"We had help," I say.

Dr. Khaled breaks the silence that followed. "I have heard of weird things happening when people work with you, but seeing the gods and goddesses come to life and an Ahmose statue march toward us and then come crashing down is unconceivable. But the worst part of all this is I can never tell anyone about it. They would never believe it." We laugh at his predicament, which is also ours.

"Maybe we can finish cataloging and transporting these artefacts to the museum in two weeks," I suggest. We need to account for cleaning and restoration after that. The process will take ages.

Finally, the work is done without incident, thank the gods.

CHAPTER FIFTEEN

ABDOULLAH, ZAHRA, NATHAN

Driving from camp to Luxor after our last day at work, we are back to reality and really hungry.

"I'm always amazed at your appetite," Abdoullah says to me.

"And I'm even more amazed at yours, my big friend."

"Something I have never made any of the sense of is why the gods wanted to help Dr. Gorman," Nathan wonders aloud. He strolls away wondering.

I try answering the question for Abdoullah, who is listening. "I think it might be because he made a pact—" I can't finish. Abdoullah is no longer listening.

"Are you all right, Abdoullah? Is it the heat?"

He doesn't answer. Just leans against me. I can't hold him, and he slowly slides down the van and falls to the ground.

"Nathan, get over here," I call to my friend, who has wandered away.

Nathan rushes over. "It's Abdoullah, I think the big guy—Do you have any pain?" I ask him.

He touches his chest and arm. He whispers something in such a quiet voice that I'm stunned.

"Hospital," I say.

We get Abdoullah in the van. Nathan drives while I call Zahra's cell. "Where's the best hospital? We have an emergency."

"There is a private hospital near to the government building, but it's expensive."

"Money doesn't matter."

We arrive in no time and Abdoullah is whisked away. Nathan and I are sitting in the waiting room when a doctor comes up to us.

"I'm glad you got here right away," the doctor says. "He had a minor heart attack, but it could be the beginning of something, or the symptom of something worse. We will do some tests, and maybe operate."

We wait for what seems like hours before a nurse comes to get us. "You can see him now. But keep it short and don't unsettle him," she says.

We follow her into a private room and see Abdoullah lying peacefully on his back.

"It's strange to see you lying here, looking pale. I hope they can get this worked out soon, my friend," I say.

"We aren't allowed to stay. We'll check on you very soon, though," Nathan assures him.

We say goodbye and walk to the station where the doctor is working. "Doctor, how is our friend, Abdoullah?"

"Well, his heart has a clogged artery. I rectified his heart problem by putting in a stent. Now we must hope for the best."

Nathan and I sneak back down the hall and into Abdoullah's room. He looks terrible. I pull the ANKH out of Nathan's backpack, hold it over Abdoullah's chest, and say the ancient chant. You never know when these things will come in handy. I say, "May you be healthy, alive and prosper," three times. The room glows a soft, healing pink. I'm sure in the supernatural mist I can sense Khepri.

We leave but check back in that evening.

"Is Abdoullah's doctor on duty?" I ask at the desk.

"No," the nurse on duty answer, "but he said to tell you a strange thing happened a short time ago. We feared Abdoullah's body was rejecting the stent as foreign. Then, it began working perfectly. He will recover."

I look at Nathan and smile. "Thanks be to Heka, God of Health, keeper of the ANKH's power."

We head to Zahra's apartment to fill her in on all that's happened when Nathan's phone rings. It's his mother. He puts her on speaker.

"Don't you boys check your phones? Nathan, you didn't get your scholarship to the American University. They didn't say why. Your grades were great—well, excellent. You were accepted, as you know, but no scholarship. Maybe you can check it out from there."

"Everything seemed to be set. I don't know what could have gone wrong." Nathan says, looking stunned. "How's everything there, Mum?" He walks away and tries to change the subject.

Zahra sits down; she is very calm. That helps a lot.

When Nathan comes back from the phone, I say, "I guess tomorrow, we're going to Cairo. After we check on Abdoullah, we can drive down to the university. Email doesn't always get to the right person."

After a night at the Susanna Hotel, we drive Abdoullah's van to the hospital.

"Can we have an update on Abdoullah? He works for us," I ask at the nurses' station. It seems strange to say it like that. Abdoullah is now a friend, not an employee.

"Abdoullah had a good night. Today we're running some tests and will be able to give you more information tomorrow. We hope we can discharge him soon."

"We must make a quick trip to Cairo, but you have my cell phone number, right?"

He confirms it's there. We thank the nurse at the desk and he smiles. They don't get thanked enough.

We drive over to the government building where Zahra takes us down to her office. Immediately, she asks, "How is he?"

"Much improved," I answer and wink.

"Okay, I'm supposed to know from your wink that your 'friend' was involved."

"We used the ANKH. Maybe my 'friend' Khepri was there." I use air quotes just like she did.

"So, we're off to Cairo," Nathan says. "Can you recommend a hotel?"

The drive is unadventurous. In the morning, we go to the American University to check on Nathan's scholarship and registration.

The very officious woman at the desk meets us. "Nathan Grant?" she asks.

"I'm Nathan Grant," he says.

"Well, we have to make sure all applications are complete. Yours is not. The high school transcript was not included, so the scholarship could not be granted."

"Didn't you have a copy when you granted us credit for field work over three months ago?"

We wait for what seems like too long. When she finally comes back, the clerk says, "Sorry for the wait. Just on a hunch, we looked in Mr. Johnsten's file and found your transcript, Mr. Grant. Yes, it was here in Mr. Johnsten's file."

"So, what are you going to do to rectify this matter?" I ask, trying very hard to remain calm and not climb over the counter. Nathan is pacing and trying not to scream.

"I don't know," she admits.

"Contact the dean of admissions and find out," I say. "We'll wait."

Shortly, the Dean himself comes out. "I'm sorry for this error, but we have already allocated all of the scholarship funds," he says.

"That sounds like disorganization and like the people on your staff are irresponsible!" I respond. I get the impression he's embarrassed, but he isn't going to let some student tell him his staff are incompetent.

I figure I'll give him a way out. "Now, if I can find someone to make a large donation to the university, could you allocate funds to cover Mr. Grant's fees? I also need to know, does the university issue an income tax receipt?"

"I'm sure we can meet both of those conditions," the dean replies.

"In the future, please ensure that more care is taken with student records."

As we walk out, I say, "Nathan, I think Dad is going to have to pay taxes on the money Mum left him. I'm sure a donation to the university would help him and you out."

I find out later that it did. Just like that.

As we come out of the building, Set is standing there in the garden, wrapped in his smoky grey cloud.

"What do you want, God of Chaos?" I challenge. His black face makes his sharp, prominent teeth vibrantly white.

"I want your Sacred Scarab and your ANKH. If you refuse, your ill friend will die."

"Try to make another threat, Set! My friend has been helped through the power of Heka!"

Set rears up to his full height, then raises his arms and his WAS sceptre. I extend my arm and my WAS sceptre appears in my outstretched hand.

"You know too much, young Jonathan! Someday, when you are weighed down in despair, I will come and collect you as a vassal of evil!" He vanishes and his cloud goes with him. My WAS evaporates as the need is over.

"Well, that was exciting for a minute," Nathan responds.

"Yep! Just stirring me up! Anyway, what are we still doing in Cairo? We're supposed to be near Luxor working on all the paperwork for the tomb of Ahmose I!" I ask and answer my own question.

So, we head for some food and drink and hit the road for Luxor. We arrive late in the evening and crash on Zahra's floor with sleeping bags.

I awake to the smell of coffee and Zahra setting out bowls and cereal. So westernized. A good-morning kiss has me thinking, *I bet my breath smells like I just slept all night with my mouth open.* I hope coffee, breakfast, and a toothbrush have helped by the time we say goodbye and she heads off to work.

***

"Are we needed here, or can we pick up Abdoullah this morning?" I ask Dr. Czerny politely at the administration tent as soon as we arrive. He gives us a couple of hours off to get Abdoullah.

We meet the doctor when we arrive. "Now your friend's problem seems to be he loves food. Perhaps you can aid Abdoullah by helping him be more careful with his diet."

"How easy will that be, do you think, Jono?" Nathan says too quickly.

"Well, he has two choices, be careful and lose his tummy, or write a will," I state.

"That, I'm afraid, is a fact," the doctor says.

We walk down the corridor to Abdoullah's room. "Hey, Abdoullah," I greet him, "you're looking great."

"My heart, she is pumping very well. But they are starving me. I am glad you are taking me out of here."

I tell him, "Well, now that you're better, the doctor says you can be released. Since it's almost noon, there's a lunch cart at the park near the government building that serves the best kushari." His eyes light up. "But you can only eat one serving!"

"Oh, I think the doctor be talking to you." He frowns.

"We want you around for a long time. That means less tummy!" I say, resisting patting it.

I give Zahra a call and she says she can meet us during her lunch break, so we get Abdoullah out of the hospital and head to the government building to meet her.

"You guys look so relaxed now that you're not in a tomb or zipping back in time," she jokes. "And you, Abdoullah are looking quite well after your ordeal."

"Zahra, be careful that someone doesn't hear you. I think Gorman has a lot of contacts. They seem to be still trying to get the-you-know-what," I caution.

"Oh, come on, Jonathan, you're being paranoid." I guess the men with guns the first time we had coffee together didn't convince her of the dangers we face.

"I hope so. Right now, I'm having very hungry, as Abdoullah says." I laugh.

"Roger that," Nathan quips.

"Now you're a pilot?" I reply.

Zahra ignore our silliness. "There's a lunch stand just around the corner by the park. They make the best kushari. Have you had it?"

"No," I respond, "but when you say it, it sounds delicious."

She continues, "Some call it the national dish of Egypt: rice, pasta, lentils, and a lot more. You can think of kushari as the best of flavours. They top it with a spiced tomato sauce and a delicious cumin sauce."

"Two sauces? It has to be good." Nathan smiles.

I don't let on that I've already told Abdoullah about her favourite cart.

We eat and find the park so relaxing with its palms and flowering shrubs after the craziness we've experienced.

"Well, Abdoullah, is it better than hospital food?" I ask.

"Yes, but I'd like more." We all give him the look. "But I know the best," he says. I wonder how long this will last. "So, Zahra, they let you out?"

"No, sir, I let myself out," she replies. "There are some perks to being your own boss."

After lunch, Abdoullah says he must meet a cousin, but I think he's just being kind. I notice he doesn't say which one. Zahra, Nathan, and I go to Zahra's apartment.

"This really is a great apartment," Nathan exclaims. "I love this patio, terrace. What do you call it?"

"It's a word we stole I think from the Italians, 'teraseena.'"

I tell her about our day. She guesses what the doctor told us and tells me about what the government is trying to do for her district. "We have quite a list of areas that need improvement. Irrigation is a top priority so that more land can be cultivated. We need more money in education but the challenges are . . . challenging," Zahra says, laughing. "What about you, Jonathan? What are your plans?"

"Nathan and I are off to AUC to select our classes. We could have done it when we were there, but the forms came by snail mail to the camp. We have quite a list of courses to choose from. Two I'm really looking forward to are 'Looking at Artefacts in Context' and 'Site Analysis.'"

Nathan ducks out. "I'll give you two some privacy. I'll be just outside having a smoke . . . except I don't smoke."

Zahra pours us a cup of coffee.

"You're such a great kisser," I tell her.

"Oh? I don't know who you're comparing me to."

"Well, I make a rule to never to kiss and tell. Can you get down to Cairo sometime soon?"

"There's a three-day weekend next month in October—Milad, the prophet's birthday."

"So tell this foreigner what happens at Milad."

I sense there is something she isn't telling me, but Nathan strolls back in. "All clear?"

"Zahra is just telling me about Milad."

"Milad, Mohammed's birthday," Zahra continues, "is celebrated with large street parades. Homes and mosques are decorated. Some people donate food and other goods to charity on or around this day."

"Does your family expect you to be at home for Milad?" I ask.

"They do, but my parents live in an area of Cairo."

"How convenient!" I laugh. I see her face become serious.

Over our coffee, Zahra says, "Jonathan, I know we love each other, but we are so different. My first language is Egyptian-Arabic, and my religion is Islam. My family has suggested a husband from a wealthy family friend. I think now is a good time for us to take a break."

I thought we were getting closer and closer. I feel like I've been hit by a bus. "But, Zahra—" She puts her hand on my mouth.

Nathan's eyes show he understands my pain. I cannot look at Zahra. Nathan and I leave.

I should have argued. I should have said, "I love you." I didn't. She had decided. It was weird, but I sensed she had made a very considered decision and I couldn't change her mind.

It's as if my world is falling apart. My mother is gone. Rex almost died. I almost lost Abdoullah. I have a conflicted relationship with Dad. And now I have lost Zahra. I can't understand it. We've become so close. Maybe if I had made love to her, things would be different. Of course, that could have made it more difficult. Yet, despite all of this, I believe in myself. I have confidence I will survive.

I need a minute to be alone. I sit on a bench in the apartment garden. I take out my mother's letter from my backpack. When I tried to read it before, I couldn't concentrate. I hope she has written something to make me feel better.

Dear Johnathan, my son,

When you read this, I will be gone. If I have any say in the matter, I will be looking down on you. I know your life will be full of trials as well as celebrations, but I raised you to be strong. I remember how you were scared, trapped in the tomb when we first went to Egypt, but you overcame that fear. I know you have loved and cared for me, and loved your father, even though you had to share him with ancient Egypt. You have loved Nathan, and I know he loves you. You are intelligent; you are resourceful. You have a powerful spirit that has enabled you to be connected to the past. I needed to write this because I did not say goodbye and I never will. I am here with you somehow.

Elizabeth, (Beth) Johnsten, your mum.

How do I feel? Well, I feel sad, teary-eyed, but proud of her and proud of myself. And so glad to have had her love.

I walk slowly out to Abdoullah's van. We're just pulling out of Zahra's apartment—I'm trying not to feel sorry for myself—when a police car drives up.

"We've been trying to track you down. We found an extensive collection of ancient pieces. We need some help identifying them. Your name is Johnsten, right?" the officer asks. He adds, "There are more pieces, hundreds of artefacts that have turned up during a raid. Could you take a look?"

"Well, I'm not qualified. Are you looking for Dr. Johnsten?"

"Look, you found the tombs. You can do this. We just want to move this stuff to the museum. If you can identify it, we can move it."

"My friends and I found treasures at Saqqara and in the Valley of the Kings. We were robbed twice."

The officer takes me into a back room of the station where there are hundreds of pieces on the table. Standing and looking at me is the golden statue of Set from Khentkaus' tomb. A memory of Nathan holding this statue in the cursed tomb flashes in my mind.

"Sir? Sir?" the officer calls me back to the present.

"Right!" I finally reply. "I know most of these definitely came from our dig. I think if you've finished using them as evidence, they should go to the Luxor Museum."

"Thanks so much," the officer says.

I walk out to the parking lot and meet up with Nathan and Abdoullah, but I only make it a few steps before the sky clouds over.

"Not again," Nathan shouts. Lightning flashes before we can we get into the van.

In front of us stand the four gods of destruction: Set, Ammit, Apep, and Shezmu. We stumble backwards, but I smirk. Set is waiting for me to be vulnerable.

I am feeling shaky, but I believe Set knows that. I know my strength and, with a bit of help, can withstand his threat.

Set snarls with his jackal teeth, Ammit snaps his great crocodile jaws, Apep rears up and hisses out his forked tongue, and Shezmu bares his bloody teeth and shakes his lion's mane. All are united against me.

Nathan, Abdoullah, and I shrink back, but the huge, long body of Apep rapidly slithers towards us and coils around the three of us. Within seconds, he brings us before Set.

"YOU HAVE DEFILED THE GRAVE OF THE KING!" Set cries. "You are in contempt of my earthly partner, Gorman. We are mighty. Do not pretend you are invincible. We are watching you plundering the god's resting places."

"We treat every piece from the Gods' tombs with respect! They will be cleaned and restored to their first beauty!" I shout back at him.

"YOU WERE NOT GIVEN PERMISSION TO SPEAK!" Set shouts. The gods close in. I'm shaking. I can feel the coils of Apep loosening until Abdoullah and Nathan are free. Then Apep rears up and his long, split tongue is literally in my face. He coils around me, choking me, more and more tightly. I can't breathe. Set laughs and thunder crashes. He shouts, "This is the end, Jonathan. I have you."

I try to pull my arm free. I can feel the WAS sceptre in my hand. I'm just able to move the end and aim it near the end of Apep's long body. When it jabs him, he shrieks and flips me into the air, into the gaping crocodile jaws of Ammit. The WAS sceptre clatters to the ground. Nathan hears and then can see it. He grabs it and stabs Ammit, who releases me, but Shezmu is ready. His lion-like fangs clamp onto my arm. Abdoullah hits him with the ANKH and he drops me like a limp rag doll. I take the WAS sceptre from Nathan and, using it for a cane, approach Set. Blood drips from my arm, but I will not be conquered.

Abdoullah has the ANKH and holds it high. I give Nathan the scarab, which glows.

"What do you want, God of Chaos?"

"We want you, Jonathan Johnsten."

"I am a strong man. I am independent. You no longer daunt me. You no longer intimidate me. I have met the Kings of Egypt and the Great Royal Wives; I have them as my support. They have given me a WAS sceptre. I have the power of this ancient Sacred Scarab. I have the sacred ANKH. Begone, harbinger of hatred, chaos, and storms. I am protected by Khepri-Ra."

I didn't know if it would be effective, but a guy has to try. I raise my right hand and with it the WAS sceptre, the long black rod with the jackal head and pronged bottom. I point it at Set.

The sky continues to darken. There is a clap of thunder and lightning forks the sky. Thunder claps and lightning forks again, this time striking the earth in front of me. Set and his companions all look at me. They recognize my strength. I keep pointing my sceptre at Set. He shakes, becomes less visible, then suddenly, he is smoke; he is gone. They are all gone!

"Wow, Jonathan, you did it! I was spooked." Nathan exclaims. "What is that rod we have?"

"This, my bro, is a WAS sceptre, held by many gods and the rulers of Egypt. It controls chaos, the chaos that has haunted me, not knowing who I am. I want my father's love, but I do not need his approval for anything I do. Now I know I am Jonathan, friend of Nathan and Abdoullah, independent, not controlled by any person but myself." I look at each of them.

"We are still here!" Set's voice whispers, repeating and repeating, "We are still here!"

Nathan, Abdoullah, and I laugh in scorn. The voice dies!

We stand in silence. I am revitalized. I can tackle anything. A familiar purple mist surrounds us. Khepri speaks as he appears. "I am here all the time, Jonathan, my son. I would not have let them kill you. I wanted you to crush Set and his minions on your own, so you would truly be a conqueror!" The mist enveloping us makes us feel exultant. We begin laughing. My arm heals as Abdoullah runs the ANKH over it and Khepri-Ra shines upon us.

"Off to Cairo!" I shout.

"Shotgun," Nathan yells, jumping into the passenger seat.

Abdoullah looks around for a robber. Nathan is in the passenger seat, and I am left to explain there is no gun involved in that crazy expression.

"When we're at the American University, we'll want you on our field study dig!" I promise Abdoullah. I hate goodbyes.

Now it's time to find a place to live, either at the dormitory or at an apartment close by. I'm driving. Nathan and I are going to university; Abdoullah is going home.

As I look out the rear-view mirror of the van, I say goodbye to Luxor and its fantastic temples, and to Saqqara, just across the Nile.

It has been a time full of magic and memories, but I'll be back.

GLOSSARY

In writing these novels I have researched the history and tried to be faithful to the research, which is changing as new tombs, documents are found.

Gods – Ammit – 'Personification of divine retribution. Devoured souls of the unworthy. Called the bone eater. Goddess, forequarters of a Crocodile, torso of a wildcat, hindquarters of a hippopotamus.

Apep – huge snake. Lived in the underworld, could bother Ra on his nightly voyage. Ate souls.

Horus – Had the head of a falcon. Son of Osiris and Isis. First king of Egypt. All kings after him believed they were Horus on Earth.

Khepri- The god wearing a beetle mask. Represented the birth of the sun, RA, or in hieroglyphs the beginning of anything. He helped the sun set and then rise again in the morning. I have used him as the God of Youth, which isn't far from new beginnings.

Khepri-Ra The connection in the above is obvious.

Set – The jackal headed god who killed his brother Osiris and lost a bet with Horus to be banished to the dessert of the west. Not a nice guy.

Shezmu- Lion headed god. Originally god of ointments, perfume, wine, and dancing. Later he became associated with blood and slaughter.

Kings of Egypt – 31 Dynasties, the Ptolemies: 14 kings. Absorbed Into the Roman Empire.

'Pharaoh' a term not used until 1200 BCE; it means 'Great House.

'Queen' there is no word in hieroglyphs, (Egyptian) for a female king, so all kings, male or female were 'king.'

The wife of a king was called 'The Great Royal Wife.' Queen was only used by non-Egyptians.

Scarab – A beetle shaped object, used to transmit information or spells.

"Scribe -- a very learned man, wrote, and read hieroglyphs. All we know about every aspect of ancient life in Egypt, from court letters, crop statistics, and so much more comes from the daily work of scribes."

WAS – the staff or sceptre with the head and feet of Anubis, Set and Khnum. Represented power and dominance over Chaos

On the map:

Giza – three famous pyramids, west of Cairo

Moving south the areas of excavation and pyramids are:

Abousir

Saqarra or Sakarra

Dahshur

Mazghuna

Itjtawy or el-Lisht

Meidum

Hawarra

ACKNOWLEDGEMENTS

The Trustees of the British Museum: permission to use the picture of the tomb painting of The pool in Fragment of a polychrome tomb-painting representing the pool in Nebamun's estate garden

Permission to use the painting: "The God Khepri" by the artist TorVik Ulloa

Special appreciation to M.D. Jackson for his cover painting for my novels.

BIBLIOGRAPHY

It is not normal to have a Bibliography for a novel, but I have researched the historical events and want readers to know how thankful I am to these writers:

Bard, K.A. (2012), An Introduction to the Archaeology of Ancient Egypt, Blackwell Publishing.

Brody, J. (2018), Save the Cat Writes a Novel, Ten Speed Press.

Budge, E.A.W. (1911), New Edition, A Hieroglyphic Vocabulary to the Theban Recension of the Book of the Dead etc., Kegan Paul, Trench, Trubner &Co. Ltd.

Desroches-Noblecourt, C., (1963), Life and Death of a Pharaoh Tutankhamen, New York Graphic Society of Ancient Egypt.

Howard, M. (2009), Egyptian Pharaohs 3,000 Years Of Dynastic Rule, Fall River Press.

Manley, B. and Collier M. A. (1998), How to Read Hieroglyphs, Amazon Canada.

Manley, B. (1996), The Penguin Historical Atlas of Ancient Egypt, Penguin Books.

Montet, P. (1964), Eternal Egypt, Phoenix Press.

Robins, G., (2008), The Art of Ancient Egypt. Harvard University Press.

Shaw, G.J., (2012), The Pharaoh, Thames and Hudson Ltd.

Shaw, I. ed., (2000), The Oxford History of Ancient Egypt, Oxford University Press.

Van De Mieroop, M., (2011), A History of Ancient Egypt, Wiley-Blackwell.

Verner, M., (2014), Sons of the Sun, Rise and Fall of the Fifth Dynasty, Charles University in Prague.

Wilkinson, T., (2013), The Rise and Fall of Ancient Egypt, Random House.

Printed in Canada